TEHRAN
AT
TWILIGHT

TEHRAN AT TWILIGHT

BY **SALAR ABDOH**

This is a work of fiction. All names, characters, places, and incidents are the product of the author's imagination. Any resemblance to real events or persons, living or dead, is entirely coincidental.

Published by Akashic Books
©2014 Salar Abdoh
ISBN-13: 978-1-61775-292-6
Library of Congress Control Number: 2014938793

First printing

Akashic Books
Twitter: @AkashicBooks
Facebook: AkashicBooks
E-mail: info@akashicbooks.com
Website: www.akashicbooks.com

Thanks to David Unger for everything.

This novel is dedicated to the memory of Hannan Dekel (b. Ostrów Mazowiecka, 1927; d. Haifa, 1993), a Tehran Child.

MALEK

He'd spent the weekend at a think tank near Dupont Circle in DC with an array of retired American military types and political science professors in and out of government service. Now, on the 1:05 a.m. train back to New York City, Reza Malek, who had once seen an angry crowd pull a man out of a Baghdad liquor shop and set him on fire, sat in a nearly empty car nursing a poorly hidden bourbon minibottle out of his laptop case, his hands slightly shaking and his mind edgy with the recollection of someone's blown-up face.

The rattle of his cell phone brought a bit of relief.

"I need you here for something." It was Sina Vafa, calling from Tehran.

"Just a minute ago I was thinking of that time in Mosul. Four years ago. Remember?"

"Three years, actually. The guy went up in the air twenty yards in front of us. When he came back down, his nose was in one place and the rest of him was, well, elsewhere."

Sina Vafa always put on a hard-boiled front, like these things didn't bother him. And maybe they didn't. But they did Malek. In fact, everything bothered Malek. He was no warrior, like Sina pretended to be. Malek was a bookworm who had found himself in the wrong war at the right time. This had made something of an academic career for him afterward. In a way the war had, strangely enough, saved his life. But he'd also seen things he'd sooner forget. Like the image of that burning man outside the liquor store over there in the Dora Quarter. Or that almost perfectly intact nose in Mosul, Iraq. One minute their handsome, young Kurdish guide, so full of life, so full of enthusiasm, was walking twenty steps ahead of them talking about his wedding plans, and the next minute he had stepped on something and his face was gone, like a mask peeled right off.

How was a guy supposed to negotiate something like that with himself? He wanted to ask Sina this. But the line had gone silent and the distant connection was cut off. So Malek's mind wandered while waiting for Sina's redial—to Mosul, to Baghdad, to Tehran, and to, of course, his best friend, Sina. Sina's hardening, his fast track to becoming such a dedicated, sworn enemy of the Americans, was something Malek had tried to put out of his mind. As if Sina's soul was just another burned corpse on the side of the road where a planted bomb had gone off.

But now Sina was calling him again. What did he want? Why call *him*? Every day Malek would wake up and read the latest body counts of young American soldiers in the news. The war was still on and each time Malek saw the reports and read the names of the dead, he sweated the way a man with a bad conscience might. He was living here in the States, but the country wasn't quite his. He was paying taxes and carried that prized blue American passport, and for two years now he'd had this plum teaching job in New York. It was an average college and he wasn't even teaching in the field he'd studied toward. But there he was, strolling over to his classes two days a week and strolling the twenty minutes back to his quiet apartment in upper Harlem. He liked his neighborhood. The staccato Spanish of the Dominicans all around him. The men playing dominoes late into the evenings on the sidewalks and the old women with their beach chairs, chattering away while little kids hollered and rode their scooters up and down the block. It was enough to give you heart and start hoping again. It made you think you could right the wrongs of the world somehow, if only you exerted yourself enough, gave yourself a chance. His own immigrant dream was right here then. And it wasn't even half bad that he was getting invitations to give his opinions to serious old men, retired warriors and Pentagon types, down there in Washington.

When the cell phone buzzed again, right away he asked Sina, "Why do you need me in Tehran?"

"I have legal issues."

"Come again?"

They spoke only English with each other. It went back to a time when they'd both been students at Berkeley, in California. There had been a point—around the beginning of their third year of college—when Malek had finally realized Sina was pretty much irredeemable. Sina had bloomed into one of those full-fledged, college-boy anti-Americans and talked about going back *East* as if that was where his salvation lay. In the very beginning, Malek had thought it was just an act. A passing stage. Every mother's son with a chip on his shoulder had to burn an American flag at least once in his life. Sina would grow out of it eventually, Malek reasoned.

And from time to time he would try to remind Sina of the plain facts: he was Sina Vafa of the famous Vafa clan, offspring of very serious Middle Eastern money. It wasn't oil money. But it was big money, nevertheless. So big and so much of it coming from Vafa's business dealings with American companies that during the revolution the Islamists had put a price on Sina's father's head. Then father and son had had to escape Iran with only the clothes on their backs. So many late-night arguments about that ugly past. The near brawls over America and the Americans. And through it all, they'd still stuck to speaking English like it was some article of faith.

"It's serious business," Sina now said, his voice turning hard. "You're the only one I trust, Rez. I need you here."

Malek considered the possibilities. "Legal issues," for a guy like Sina, in a place like the Islamic Republic, could really only mean one thing: Sina had finally managed to convince the courts to give some of his father's confiscated assets back to him. The holdings were so vast—factories, chains of restaurants, land, sports teams, movie houses, and swaths of forest near the Caspian Sea shore—that even a fraction of that estate still meant an unimaginable fortune. But this brought up other questions: Why should the Islamic Republic give anything back to Sina? What had he done to convince them he deserved some of his godless, America-loving father's estate back? And where was Malek's place in all of this?

For a moment Malek balked, silently. It wasn't that he'd promised himself he'd never go back. It was just that there was nothing for him to go back to over there.

Except Sina. He sensed a trap. Legal issues meant getting involved. They meant putting your name and signature on things. Malek's unease made him consider his whiskey bottle for a second. In the train car, men and women were dozing behind their laptops. Business travelers. Their lives reasonably comfortable, except for these odd-hour train rides and early flights between the coasts. Maybe they had second homes up there in Westchester or down in the Chesapeake. No doubt they had their own troubles too. But nobody was ever going to ask them to come to a place like Tehran and get involved in legal matters. What legal matters? Over there, it was *their* way or the jail cell. But he couldn't say no, could he? And once he realized he couldn't say no, a cloud lifted. His old friend wasn't beyond changing. He would go to Tehran and bring Sina back from the cold.

Yet he knew better than to try to get any more information from Sina over a phone line between Tehran and this moving train chugging north across the state of Delaware. Feeling himself already falling in deep, and with a voice that probably betrayed it, he answered, "Summer vacation is almost here. I'll come back, brother. Let us talk then."

Back in New York, Malek had a few hours of sleep before the phone woke him up. It was Clara Vikingstad. Contrary to the girth of that last name, Clara was a small woman. A brunette in her late forties with intelligent brown eyes that saw the world mostly in terms of not being denied her will. Malek had spent a good portion of his adult life chasing a PhD in Middle Eastern studies. Yet of all the people he'd ever met in the business, Clara

had a special way with the region. She had an ambition
to match that too. She had saved Malek's behind, literally, in Baghdad in the spring of 2004. And for that he
would always owe her.

"It was good seeing you again, Rez," she said. "I
want to propose something to you."

"Let me guess, you're going back to Tehran and you
need an interpreter."

"Who better than you?"

He'd be glad to oblige, he told her. In Baghdad she
had flexed all of her 5'1" frame and stood up to that over-
zealous US Army staff sergeant who had thought Malek
was acting suspicious: "That's my translator you are arresting and I won't let you do it." And when the man
had tried to shove her out of the way and ordered a
couple of his amped-up nineteen-year-olds in uniform
to take *hajji* away, she'd bluffed that this story would be
prime time news eight hours later in America. By then
she was screaming—"And that, my friend, will be the
end of your shining military career!" It was enough to
get Malek off the hook. Enough to start him loving her
for it. Yet a couple of years later, back in the States, he
had quickly become just another source for her, just another interpreter, another guy Clara had worked with in
some messy corner of the world for a while. Malek was
a number, a face, a local guy you slept with a few times
because the sound of not-so-distant mortars was amaz-
ingly conducive to casual sex.

Did all this mean he resented her? By God, no. He
was the willing *dust under her feet*, as the Persians said.
She had done him a solid once, and no, he would not
forget it.

He said, "You know, Clara, I've been following your latest articles. But really, what's in Guatemala for you?"

"Death squads. Kidnappings. The usual stuff. I just had to get out of the Middle East for a while, Rez. You know how that is. You did the same." After a pause she said, "I'm sorry I couldn't talk to you more over the weekend."

She had been a guest at that think tank too. But she'd come with a man. An older, suavely condescending photojournalist who apparently was in the pantheon of his profession. One of those salt-and-pepper Hemingway types whose résumés say they've covered three dozen wars in 140 countries and they don't mind you knowing all about it.

Still, Malek had had dinner with them Saturday night and Clara had said she'd call. And so she had.

"It's all right," he said, "we'll have plenty of time to talk in Tehran. Unless His Majesty, your photographer friend, is coming there with you."

She laughed. "He's just a friend. And anyway, the Iranians won't give him a visa."

"They want you all to themselves, Clara," he joked tiredly, "and I can't say I blame them."

In Washington, she'd asked what he was up to these days and he'd told her he'd settled into that teaching job in New York.

"Well, it looks like you landed on your feet in America, Rez. It beats chasing stories, always worried about your next job, doesn't it? You've found your niche here. Stick to it."

Once more he thought of how in Clara's line of work you came upon people that you gigged with for a bit;

sometimes the intimacy became exaggerated because of circumstance, like that spring in Baghdad. You worked together, you slept together, and then, once an assignment was finished, you went your separate ways. Maybe you stayed in contact for a period. But life took over and the contact became pale. It was what it was. Even affairs were on a fast clock that way.

"It's true, it's a safe job, Clara. I don't know how long it will last, though."

"Why?"

"They insist I write another book."

She laughed again, this time like he'd said something dumb. "Rez, that's what you're supposed to do when you assume the title of *professor*. How many years did you go to school for that?"

"And if I don't write one, and soon, they'll shake my hand and say it was nice having you here. They needed a resident *sand negro* for a while," he said, emphasizing the words for effect. "Maybe to fill their hiring quotas. Now that they've filled it—"

"Stop that talk, Rez. You sound like a nag."

"Clara," he persisted, "I was, you know, kind of liking my life lately. It's simple. It's peaceful. You'll hear a gunshot now and then in my neighborhood. But no RPGs, no IEDs. It's a veritable Eden up here in Harlem. I don't want to lose it. I really, really don't."

"You won't. But if worse comes to worst, you can always head down to Washington and work for one of these think tanks. God knows there's enough of them. I could even put in a good word for you. I got connections."

She was being kind. Her kindness was real.

"You mean I could sit in some cubicle every day and

churn out report after report for washed-out colonels and generals while the world burns?"

"The world is always burning, Rez. Don't take it so personal."

After she hung up, he spent a long time going over the two phone conversations he'd had that day. Clara Vikingstad wanted him to come to Tehran and be her translator again, and Sina wanted him to come for *something*. That city, Tehran, was like a lost, confused, and very dangerous kid to Malek. And it grew and grew all the time. It got fat in every direction and didn't know its own right hand from its left. It was a place of mostly quiet desperation but also grand stupid gestures that went nowhere. After a while there, you just got tired of slugging it out every day for every little thing. And one day you woke up and realized that you had forgotten how to smile. You watched the bleakness on the long black *chadors* of the religious women and you felt you couldn't breathe. Conversely, you were invited to the parties of the rich where every kind of vice was to be had for a song, and you felt like you could breathe even less. The mania of it all, the lopsidedness of a city that entertained in its contours every level of danger that could be bought, became too much after a while. You wanted to escape then. But by now Tehran had become an addiction. It held you down. Certainly it had held Malek for a time. And he was afraid of the place. Afraid because he knew it too well; knew how things could turn on you in a heartbeat. And then you were in too deep and there was no one and nowhere to turn to.

Candace Vincent was in his office.

It had begun three months earlier. The beginning of the spring semester. She had come to the office one day asking for his help. "Professor, I want to soar. I want to write about my hood like it really is." She wanted to keep it *real*, she insisted. Write about how it was to be a single black woman, just shy of thirty, raising two little boys in her public housing apartment in the projects across the river in the Bronx. Would he help her? Would he give her guidance once in a while?

It was odd that she'd come to him for this kind of mentoring. It wasn't exactly a part of his job description. But all right, yes, he'd read her stuff. And they didn't have to be just class assignments. He'd make corrections. Give suggestions. "I'm available to you, Candace." But, really, it was more for himself that he was doing it. Helping this student was, he decided, the point where he'd start to make a new life for himself here, in America. You had to start somewhere, and why not with Candace Vincent? And so for three months he had been reading about the minutiae of her life—the drama of dropping her kids at school every morning, then the ordeal of waiting and waiting at a half-dozen government offices any given week for food stamps, benefit cards, housing, health insurance. A never-ending merry-go-round of hustle and bureaucracy that reminded him of how people lived back in Tehran. A world removed from his own but also familiar. And slowly, an unlikely distant camaraderie had blossomed out of this back and forth. One that was pure. It didn't ask for much except to be at the other side of an e-mail exchange.

But now it was nearing the end of the school year and Candace was in his office again, worried that since she would no longer be his student, he'd forget her and not want to read what she had to write.

"Will you let me keep e-mailing you my work, professor?"

"Of course."

She looked away and said, "My two boys' pops is getting out of jail soon."

"Is it a good thing or a bad thing that your man's getting out?"

She shook her head. "He ain't been my man for a long time. Just my babies' father. I don't know if it's good or bad. We'll see about that. But whatever happens, you can be sure I'll write to you about it."

He stood up and she came forward and gave him a big, warm, sisterly hug. She pulled back, looked at him, and said, "You are all right in my book, professor."

He told her the feeling was mutual.

Then a half hour later Malek was waiting outside of the head of the English department's office.

In his e-mail, the department head had written that it was urgent he see Malek before the faculty scattered for the summer. Now the man stuck his head out of the office, saw Malek sitting there, and made a motion for him to come in. He was one of those bouncy little administrators too full of jittery enthusiasm. Malek would often see him in the far-flung wings of the building checking to see if the plants in other departments had enough water. It had been exactly three years earlier that he'd received an e-mail from this guy on behalf of the college asking, out of the blue, if he'd be interested in joining their faculty as a resident journalist. It was to be a one-year trial, and if things worked out they might renew Malek's contract from year to year. After five years, there would even be the possibility of a permanent position.

Even before Malek had sat down, the department head asked, "Do you think you might publish something next year?"

"I'm working on it."

"What does that mean?" The man's voice sounded hurt, like Malek had wronged him. He was a Texan with an unusually high voice. His disappointment needed focus and Malek's failure to publish even one article about the Middle East in the two years he'd been there gave him an opportunity to pout a little. "I brought you here because I saw promise in the book you wrote. I fought to get you this residency."

It hadn't really been a book. More like a patchwork of reports from the sidelines of America's wars, and Malek had come upon it mostly by chance. After Berkeley, it had taken him another seven years to complete that doctorate in Middle Eastern studies. Seven years of studying a school of Sufis, Muslim mystics, who had lived in Basra, in modern-day Iraq, a thousand years ago. Mystics who went on endlessly about how God's light shone on everything and everyone. Not that that was a useless thing to study (somebody had to do it, Malek supposed), but the year was 2002 when he'd gotten that degree, America was already in Afghanistan and was getting ready to go into Iraq, and there weren't exactly a whole lot of universities looking to hire someone to tell them about the Muslim mystics of a thousand years ago. So he'd packed up and returned home. Sina had already been living back in Tehran for some years and when Malek got there his old friend helped him pick up interpreter jobs until Malek was on his feet and had his own clients, journalists who came for their rounds from time to time, people like Clara Vikingstad. The years of graduate work had honed Malek's Arabic too, so he had turned out to be that rare interpreter who could carry a Western reporter not just in Iran and Afghanistan, but also Iraq and other Arab countries. After a while he was an interpreter in high demand, his name in the address book of every foreign correspondent between Berlin and Los Angeles. This way he'd gotten to see his share of the *interesting* and slowly started writing little reports on the side and having them published in Asian newspapers and online. Before long, somebody somewhere had gotten wind of the material and offered to put them out in a collection. There had been a couple of fair reviews online. And then out of nowhere this Texan with the high nasally voice had written him an e-mail, asking if Malek was interested in joining their department to teach students how to do *creative reportage*. Malek's take was: *Why not?* Living in Tehran and moving around constantly in that region was getting to be tiresome anyway. Eventually you just got bogged down in the details. Another suicide bombing. Another high-level assassination. Another missed unmanned drone missile that killed forty members of a family in the middle of a wedding. You became cynical and then you became self-conscious of your own cynicism and posed for it. It was a bad cycle. Bad enough that Malek had already started toying with the ever-present opium between Tehran and Kabul.

Yes, he would go back to America and teach creative reportage, whatever that was. The Texan's offer was a godsend, a lifeline. And considering that including his undergraduate years Malek had studied more than a decade about those Muslim mystics, maybe it was some sweet poetic justice that he was finally being offered an academic job. He'd earned it.

"I'm working on something now," he now said to the department head. It was an outright lie. He had nothing. He had put that book together because he happened to be in the middle of those wars and simply recorded what he saw. He wasn't a Clara Vikingstad or any of the others he'd done interpreting for. He wasn't a pro. He had written because he was a witness. There was a difference.

The man took several pills of varying colors from a pillbox on his table and downed them all at once as if they were candy. He then took a swig from his coffee and eyed Malek. "There's another matter." Malek waited for him to spit it out. "We're hiring someone else on the same lecture-line as you. He's coming in September."

So that was the real reason he had been called in here today. The department head had wanted to break the news to him that they were hiring someone else to compete for the permanent teaching position.

He didn't really know what to say to the man. In a way, it was generous of him to let Malek know this. This was a "heads-up" kind of meeting. *You better write something new about that Middle East of yours, Professor Malek. Or you're history.* "I'd like to meet this person," Malek said, just to have said something. "My new colleague."

The department head suddenly brightened. Maybe it was the pills working quickly. "I tell you what." He fished in his desk and brought out a book. *Winter in Babylon.* Author, James McGreivy. "It's a fantastic book. This is what your new colleague wrote. It covers some of the same things your book does. Well, not really. The man's a former Marine captain. Iraq, Afghanistan, all that. It's a good book. It might inspire you. You should read it."

"I already did."

The department head looked stung, as if the notion that Malek would actually read other books was beyond him. He said, "Well, what did you think of it?"

"It's brilliant."

"How so?"

"It has truth." Then to really rub it in, Malek added, "I've even used parts of it to teach my own classes."

By the time Malek left that office, the English department had taken on the festive air of end-of-year celebrations. There were wine bottles lined up and young, underpaid graduate-student teachers were drifting in to eat from the generous spread laid out on the long table. Malek stood there for a moment watching. The first year, not sure if his contract was just going to be temporary, he had mostly stayed a stranger to the place, keeping a low profile and sticking to the classes he had to teach. The full professors, he knew mostly through what they taught, the Shakespearean, the Americanist, the Victorian, and so on. But this past year—maybe because the department head was putting pressure on him—he'd begun to pay more attention. He came to the faculty meetings, sat in the back, and listened. There were factions, he'd noticed. They fought. Mostly over nothing. It was an arrangement of low-key corruption where the department head and his cronies had the run of the place. They gave each other promotions and assigned themselves light teaching loads and generally had a ball with the little fiefdom they had going. As soon as Malek understood this scheme, he accepted it. The department head may have been just slightly dishonest, but at least he wasn't killing people. In Baghdad, Malek had watched a whole neighborhood go up in flames over who'd get to inherit the electric generator the Americans had left behind by mistake. One was a world of flesh and blood, the other of text and ink and boredom and irrelevance.

He wondered how Captain James McGreivy of the United States Marines would fare here next fall. The fellow really *had* written a good book about the war. But what had possessed him to give up all that adrenaline and want to come to a place like this just to teach? How would he be able to stand it?

The thought made Malek revisit something that had happened the previous semester. There had been a Latino kid in one of his classes, Ezequiel. "Call me Easy," he'd told Malek. Easy had done all right in class for the first few weeks. Always polite, always on time and handing in lukewarm pieces he'd written about not much of anything. Then one day, out of nowhere, he'd written of how he'd done a part of his New York State National Guard tour of duty out of Base Speicher near Tikrit in Iraq:

Do you know, professor, what a fifty-caliber machine gun can do to a family of four Iraqis who didn't see your hand signal to turn their car around? I looked you up the other day online, man. I saw some of the stuff you wrote. YOU KNOW how it was over there. But you stand here and smile at these dumbasses in your class like the world is all fine

and dandy and we should all go to the mall in New Jersey
and buy Christmas gifts. You think that's honest? You and
your kind, you ain't shit, professor. This whole place ain't
shit. This country ain't shit.

The kid had been all of twenty-five years old, and
he had perfect spelling, and he'd never come back to
Malek's class after writing him that note. Malek had
waited for his return, unwilling to drop him from the
class roster until the very end. And for the rest of those
weeks he'd walked these hallways expecting some sort
of bad news about the kid and vaguely blaming himself
for it.

You and your kind, you ain't shit, professor.

The following semester he had taken Candace Vincent under his wing—Candace, who knew nothing of
the war but could sometimes write like an angel.

SINA

Malek sat in a tea shop on Orumiya Street in Tehran watching the traffic flow. The tea shop was heavy with the sound of Azeri Turkish and the smoke from smoldering *qilyans*. The place was small, packed with bodies, and permeated with the stale scent of labor and tolerable poverty. It was nothing like those touristy hookah places in Istanbul or Cairo or even Damascus where men might sit for hours playing backgammon and chatting leisurely into the wee hours of the night. Across the street a bike rider came to a stop at Vafa Alley. But it wasn't Malek's man. Malek hunkered down, even though he was allergic to the smoke. He wasn't going to find a better place to keep watch.

He was startled when he heard his name called. The man had somehow entered unnoticed and slipped in across the long bench from Malek. Gray suit. Short beard. Recent haircut. He didn't seem like *Ettelaat*, Intelligence, but it was a given he had plenty acquaintances in that world. He had the look not of a shark but a lawyer. There was a slight difference. Malek had known men like him. They were comfortable in their own skin. The Islamic Revolution had been good to them. They knew where the connections lay. They were men who didn't need to interrogate; they could sweet-talk.

Malek said, "I don't know what I'm doing here, to be honest."

"You're keeping an eye on your friend Sina Vafa's house."

"I know that. Mr. . . . ."

"Fani."

"But I'm not sure why I'm doing it. I mean, I have a decent enough life far away from here, in America, as I'm sure you know."

"What is decent about it?"

"Well, I don't have to watch anybody's house before I go say hello. Especially my best friend's house."

"It could have to do with the circumstances."

"What are those?"

He expected Fani to say that it was Malek's job to tell him that. But Fani just eyed him with an amused look. He was obviously enjoying this: two men who had never met until this moment could sit in this teahouse and speak like old friends or adversaries. It was a world of double meanings and casual one-upmanship and it was about as far away from his life in New York as one could get. Malek gauged Fani's face and realized that the man had decided to like him, for now. It was that simple; Fani would have enjoyed this back and forth with anyone who had the presence of mind not to get spooked so easily. Another guy might have fallen to pieces had Fani approached him so suddenly. But Malek knew how to hold ground. Other things rattled him. But not this.

Fani did a survey of the tea shop and Malek's eyes followed him. Such a world of men it was. The stink of men, Malek thought to himself. That was the other difference—in New York he moved in a world tilted toward women. Most of his students, like Candace, were women. So were the clients in the physical therapy class he had started taking in Chelsea to heal his bad back from that bus crash in Afghanistan's Badakhshan Province four years earlier. Had there been just one woman amongst all these men here, the place would have had a different feel. And suddenly Malek felt nostalgic, as if he were never going to see women again, and he had to pull himself out of this silly reverie and collect his thoughts for the next phase of sparring with Fani.

Fani said, "Sina Vafa has called you to Tehran. There's a reason for that. Do you know the reason?"

"How do you know I haven't come of my own free will? Anyway, shouldn't we be having this conversation in a small, nondescript hotel room downtown?"

Fani laughed and loudly ordered a round of tea for himself and Malek.

"This *is* downtown, Mr. Malek. Do you know the reason why your friend called you?"

"No."

"In 2004 and 2005 you took several trips to Iraq and Afghanistan. A few of those trips you went with Mr. Vafa."

"I didn't know it would interest anyone."

"What did you do in the places you went?"

Malek turned to his right and left, imagining men were listening in on their conversation. But nobody was. The TV was on and for a moment a newscast showed the Iranian president giving a speech somewhere. A loud voice in Turkish called the president a "whore's son" and someone else asked to turn the "fool's" mug off that television screen.

"I was working with journalists. So was Sina. We

came and went. Sometimes together, sometimes not. It was an interesting time. That's about it."

"It's still an interesting time over there."

"I'm done with all that."

"But your friend continues those trips."

"Maybe he's still working with foreign journalists."

Fani gave Malek a look. *Do you take me for a fool?* He asked, "Do you know of QAF?"

How could he not know? QAF was the shortened name of an outfit in Tehran, with a newspaper as a front, that was about as reactionary as you could get. These were guys who didn't suggest the cutting off of the heads of infidels; they demanded it.

"I am not going to believe you telling me Sina Vafa has been working with QAF."

"Why? Because you don't want to? Or because you believe that QAF would never accept someone of Sina Vafa's *dirty* background?"

"Both those reasons. Besides, what does Sina's going to Iraq have to do with QAF?

Another incredulous look from Fani. And then he said, "Ask these questions of your friend yourself, Mr. Malek." He smiled and got up.

"Is that it?" Malek asked, surprised. He had expected all sorts of revelations. Or even offers. It was routine. Part of the trade. During the time he worked with the foreign journalists, he'd been called into the Intelligence Ministry, was served tea, and then they showed photographs of him with various reporters, including Clara Vikingstad. He'd been asked if he wouldn't mind working with their bureau. There had been no pressure, though. It was simply procedure—*You work with foreigners,*

we want to know what they're up to. They'd even had pictures
of him and Clara in Beirut and Amman. Both side trips
that had been more out of curiosity than work. If anything was going to rattle him, it would have been that.
But even then he'd kept his cool. He'd just as politely
said no, he wasn't interested. And they hadn't pressed
it any further. The guys in Intelligence knew their job.
They had asked if he wanted more tea and then gave him
their spiel—*Contact us if you ever change your mind.* A couple
of years later, he'd been called in again. This time they
knew he'd published a book though they weren't un-
happy about it. In fact, they were kind of pleased. They
already knew he was going to teach in a college in New
York and asked him if his answer was still no. He had
wanted to tell them, *I'm going to New York to teach creative
reportage, for Christ's sake. What is it you think I can do for you
over there?* But to these men the world was always one
of seized opportunities and missed ones. They told him
that the public college he'd be teaching at was where a
lot of Iranian UN consulate staff sent their kids because
they couldn't afford the expensive private schools. What
they had essentially been asking him was to keep a tab
on the children of their own diplomatic corps in New
York. It was obscene. And made perfect sense.

Fani said, "You can tell Sina Vafa that you saw me.
Or, if you like, you don't have to. We'll meet again."

"About what?"

"There are many things for us to meet about."

The sound of bodybuilders and local toughs came from
a large basement where a gym had been rented out by
the Vafa clan. The building was one of theirs, an old,

badly kept property that the revolution hadn't bothered to claim from Sina's family. Sina's apartment was on the third floor. A nearly barren living room with just a wooden writing desk in a corner that had its legs sawed off. The only other things were a laptop and a dozen pillows of varying sizes and colors scattered about. Glancing into the bedroom, Malek saw mostly books, which at first glance weren't a bad sign.

Sina appeared healthy and must have been hitting the weights regularly. His muscles taut and buffed, his face a repository of blankness that comes from overexerting your body. His dark skin was also weathered and tanned and he had a week-old beard. What he looked like was a stranger. He could have been one of those wrestlers making humphing noises in the basement.

He asked Malek if he wanted tea.

"I've had plenty today."

"How many cups did Fani have?"

Malek took the jab from Sina in stride.

Sina went on, "Look, the tea shop owner is my friend. He told me Fani visited you there. But don't worry about that. Fani *wanted* to be seen at the teahouse."

"I don't get the logic of any of this, Sina."

"Why should you? I don't mind if you stake out my place before you come and ring the buzzer. I might have done the same. It's procedure. Our lives are permanent emergency in this part of the world."

"You exaggerate. You just want it to be that way. It makes you feel important."

"And what if it does? In America I was a zero. A nothing. But in this city I call my own shots, make my own plans."

Here it was, the same old tired arguments, and Malek saw himself falling right into the trap, yet couldn't keep himself from sounding off: "Don't lie to yourself, man. If you want to have your adventures, go ahead and have them. But don't blame the problems of the world on America or neocolonialism or whatever other bullshit they tried to slam down our throats in college, or in those books you got in your bedroom."

"One of the books in my bedroom, Rez, is yours. Not a bad book either. I didn't think you had it in you to actually write a book."

Malek hated these conversations. But still he couldn't back out. Sina had called him to Tehran and he had come. But he hadn't come unconditionally. He had questions. They were questions that he should have asked years ago—though that would have meant sticking around in this godforsaken city.

But now he simply wanted to get drunk. Maybe he just wanted his old friend back. The Sina of their college years. He wanted them to be sitting outside a café on Telegraph Avenue in Berkeley, talking politics while sipping strong black coffee and sneaking whiskey into their cups. There was so much water under the bridge and so much had turned to shit. Think of all the fixers and translators and interpreters and drivers and typists and snitches and local reporters who had worked in and out of the Green Zone in Baghdad, all of them waiting for their visas to the good old United States, visas that were delayed for years or were never approved, those impossible stamps of transit that would save them from getting killed in reprisal by their own countrymen who thought them traitors—think of all those poor bastards

West Vancouver
MEMORIAL LIBRARY

Items that you checked out

Title: Tehran at twilight / by Salar Abdoh.
ID: 31010001829748
Due: August-01-18

Items checked out this session: 1
July-11-18
Checked out: 1
Overdue: 0
Hold requests: 0
Ready for pickup: 0

Renew 604-925-7404 or
http://wvml.ca/renew
Mon-Thu 10-9 Fri 10-6 Sat 10-5 Sun 10-5
(Closed Sundays July-August)

in hiding now, and why not thank our lucky stars that both of us carry American passports? He wanted to tell Sina all this and, most importantly, he wanted to tell him to drop it all, drop whatever he had gotten himself into, and just return with him stateside. And, of course, he knew what Sina would say to that suggestion: *What's a darkie like me supposed to do over there?*

"I need a drink," Malek said.

"None in my house."

"Why? Because you work for QAF now and if they found out you got alcohol in your place they'd be disappointed? You'd no longer be a good little Muslim in their eyes?"

"Fani told you about QAF, did he?"

"Did you expect he wouldn't? What are you thinking, Sina? QAF are the kind of people who put your father on a death list. They're the ones who forced you and your old man into exile in the first place. They tell poor bastards once they get up there to heaven they're sure to have red-lipped maidens waiting to welcome them. This is not my imagination. It's real. Just go online and see how they got entire websites devoted to this sort of garbage. And you're a part of it. Why are you working for them?"

"I only translate."

"You lie!" Malek shouted this. But at least the tension that had been building finally broke. Here they stood in the middle of Tehran, two Americans. When you really got down to it, that was what they were. Even their accents, Malek noted, were nondescript California.

Nothing made sense, of course. It was the way this place was, a place of nonmeaning. This was what Malek had dreaded, that he'd come here and enter wonderland again. Take QAF, for instance. It was like the organization existed and didn't exist. Sure, in the newspapers abroad you read about special-operation units of the Revolutionary Guards operating in Iraq. They were doggedly trained and had agents running things everywhere. But QAF was something entirely different. It was more a shadowy nonorganization of radical clerics, newspapermen, archconservative bazaar merchants, dangerous dreamers, and current and former officers who were convinced the Messiah was on His way. They didn't advertise themselves, but you knew they were there. More than anything, they were an inspiration to others. They gave direction. Tried to keep the fire of the aging revolution hot. You couldn't point to one guy and say, *That's QAF*. QAF was a state of mind more than anything, and yet it had its tentacles everywhere.

And maybe that was why it suited a guy like Sina so well. Sina was a child of the old aristocracy. He couldn't have gotten a job with the regular military or any of the competing intelligence agencies even if his life depended on it. They wouldn't trust him. They knew him for what he was, an American when it came right down to it. But people also knew just how rich the Vafa family had been. The kind of money that knocked the wind out of you. In every major thoroughfare in Tehran alone, there were properties that had belonged to Vafa. And even now, whoever managed to get any sort of a claim on that level of fortune would have enough cash to run operations for years and years without having to go begging at the state coffers.

Sina was a tool. He had been made into one or had

volunteered for the job of being one. This made him dangerous, pathetic, courageous, and absurd all at the same time. It made him a right fit for Tehran. Where else in the world could you imagine a guy like him going about his business as he did here? Sina was two of everything—a rich/poor, revolutionary/antirevolutionary, religious/irreligious, Iranian/American, who rode a motorcycle on the streets of Tehran and could point to a good portion of the city and say *that* and *that* and *that* had belonged to his daddy.

An hour later they had parked Sina's motorcycle near a three-star hotel on Taleqani Avenue. Several Venezuelan policemen and bodyguards from a visiting oil delegation sat around bored to death in the lobby, without booze and without women. Their diplomats were elsewhere, probably being wined and dined, and there was nothing for these guys to do except sit there and look like they might shoot somebody. But in the basement of that hotel, Malek and Sina entered a dark empty breakfast room, and without so much as four words exchanged, a man came out from the kitchen with a tray of vodka and two shot glasses.

Malek knew better than to ask. Everywhere Sina went in this town, he probably had half-invisible men who had once worked for his father now doing favors for him. The two men drank a good portion of the bottle without much talking. Outside, they could hear revolutionary songs being piped very loudly out on the street. That was from the old American embassy that had been stormed by the crowds during the revolution some twenty-eight years earlier. For a long time the place had served as a kind of museum to American infamy. *Nest of Spies*, they had called it.

Sina said, "I have to go away for about a week."

"What are you doing for QAF, Sina?"

"They're just a newspaper."

"Where are you going for a week?"

Sina shrugged. "I could tell you anything, couldn't I? I could tell you I got a story to report about down by the Gulf. Or that I have to go to Islamabad to translate for a bunch of fat Iranian middlemen who want to sell the Pakistanis stolen gas."

"But you're not doing either of those things."

He waited for Sina to open up and say something really worth flying six thousand miles for. But then, with a few shots of vodka in him, Malek had a revelation. Two people could come to a point where they either had to kiss and make love or the thing that was between them would turn awkward and stale. It was like that now. If Sina didn't give him a hint of what he was up to, then they had nothing more to do with each other. It was over. Maybe Sina felt some of that too, because now he said, "I'll take you part of the way with me where I'm going this week. How's that?"

"Why would you do that?"

"Because," Sina took a long pause, "just like that guy Fani wanted to be seen at the tea shop, now I don't mind him seeing you come all the way to the border with us."

"Iraq?"

Sina nodded.

"You want him to think I'm protected so he will lay off of me, because by laying off of me he's really laying off of you?"

"Yes."

"But protected from what?"

"I'll tell you that part of it when I come back from the other side."

"And what's happening on the other side?"

"It's the Wild West over there. And I'm loving it."

"Sina, why do this? What have the Americans done to you?"

Folding over his shot glass, Sina muttered, "They piss on us and say, *Smile! It's raining.*"

The vodka was really going to Malek's head. The oval-shaped basement breakfast room was like something you might see on a retiring cruise ship, its paint peeling and the carpeting musty and worn. The place had probably seen far better days when the American embassy had been across the street and functioning. Malek waited while Sina whistled and the silent waiter came out of the shadows again and brought some yogurt and cucumbers.

Now Malek was having himself a second revelation: you act a part long enough, eventually you come to be trapped in it. In college, Sina had been just another snot-nosed twenty-year-old with a chip on his shoulder, going to anarchist rallies at People's Park in Berkeley and shouting all that *Down with US imperialism* nonsense. But somewhere along the line, in the years that he'd been here, that little college boy had hardened into something else. It was like the promise of a marriage you can't back out of. This was his role and what he lived to do. For Malek, who was but a few days removed from his teaching job back in New York, the thought was macabre. Here was a man getting drunk with him whose purpose in this world had probably reduced itself to this: taking down one poor, overburdened farm boy from, say, Wisconsin or Minnesota, with an M16 and a hundred pounds of gear on his back, at a time. And he would do it wherever he could—the Anbar Province, the Kunar; wherever there was a pasty-faced kid with an accent not unlike his own.

The thought, along with the alcohol, made Malek want to cry like a fool. He recalled the road trips he and Sina used to take together in college. Often they'd go down to towns like Bakersfield and hit the bars with Sina's guitar and ten-gallon cowboy hat in tow. Sina had looked like some smashed Mexican cowboy out to prove himself better than the white man at his own game. He could belt those country songs like few could. Offering such aching renditions of "Lost Highway" that even those disbelieving truckers and barflies would come up to him afterward and shake his hand or buy him drinks. It didn't seem like another lifetime ago. It was more like it had never happened; it had been a dream.

Malek pushed the last of his drink aside. His misery just then was total and he wouldn't have minded breaking something and going upstairs to pick a fight with those Venezuelan bodyguards. *Somewhere along the line we turned into killers. We all did. You fuckhead, Sina! You fuckhead for dumping your world on me like this.*

Sanandaj. Iranian Kurdistan. Malek sat in an outdoor ice-cream shop off of Abidar Street. Kurdish men wearing baggy *shalwars* gave him curious looks that were neither suspicion nor dislike. Just the curiosity of men whose pride was as sharp as their knives. He had forgotten how beautiful nature was out here. No wonder that Kurds, Iranians, Turks, Iraqis, even Syrians all wanted a piece of it. When it wasn't bleeding, Kurdistan could be postcard-perfect. For Malek, there was also that old feeling of going on a job, as when you are about to cross a border, on foot, illegally, not sure if you'll return. He was even tempted to look up some contacts from times past, runners and guides he had known who regularly took black-market goods between Sanandaj within one border to Sulaimaniyah on the other side.

But roughing it like that, Malek now saw, was something that took staying in the game; it took practice, it was a language you had to speak a little every day lest you forgot it. Here, he felt a bit too old and shut out by Sina. He craved his own bed and a strong cup of coffee.

"You drove me all the way out here so I can take a bus by myself back to Tehran?"

"Sure. It'll give you time to think about the two things I want to tell you."

"So tell me."

"I want to give you a full power of attorney. I want you to be my legal agent in case I'm not around."

The sheer scale of what Sina was asking stunned Malek. To have a full power of attorney in Iran from someone of Sina's background meant trouble. It meant attention would suddenly be directed Malek's way. He would be the one answerable for Sina's presumed estates—estates that could, theoretically, be returned to him if the revolutionary courts decided to favor him one day. And Sina being an only heir, that could translate to *everything*. Every single piece of land, idle factory, and deserted restaurant his father had owned.

He thought, *I could get up from here, say no, and be on my way.* They had had a longtime comradeship that transcended all their disagreements and distance. But this? Dumping on Malek a power of attorney when they were only a few miles away from the border, and on the other side lay Iraq in flames and who the hell knew what Sina was up to over there . . . and then for him to add, *in case I'm not around* . . . Why wouldn't he be around? What was supposed to happen to him? Malek knew better than to accept. He didn't owe that kind of favor to Sina. Not here, not like this. But all he could bring himself to ask was, "You want to give me a power of attorney so I can do what for you?"

"Just say you'll accept. We'll talk about the details later."

Malek looked down at his shoes and then back up and met Sina's gaze. "I accept."

Sina's face relaxed and went soft. As if Malek had just given him a new lease on life. They stayed silent for a while.

Then Malek sighed. "Look, I can't read your mind. You said you had two things to tell me."

"I have an address." Sina paused. "An address for your mother."

"Come again?" Malek had not heard from nor thought much about his mother in three decades. He waited for Sina to go on, trying to appear indifferent and not succeeding much at it. Was this some kind of joke? "What's my mother got to do with anything?"

"Nothing. I just thought you might like to know where she is. I know you haven't seen her since before the revolution. I thought—"

"You thought you were asking your old pal to do you a favor by accepting a power of attorney from you in this hellhole and you wanted to do him a favor in return?"

"Well, yeah."

"Where is she then?" Despite trying to control himself, Malek felt his pulse racing a little. "I mean, does she have an address near a beach in Australia or something?"

"No, she has an address far from a beach in Tehran."

The bus was mostly Iraqi Shias and Kurds who were going to Tehran for care because there weren't enough doctors and hospitals in their own areas. A busload of Iraqis of every age in various stages of blindness, their faces perfectly masked with resignation to their illness. It was maddening to watch. And as the light gave way, Malek felt he wanted to do their seeing for them.

He thought back to Sanandaj and the mention of his mother, Soaad. One day when he was twelve years old, his old man had come home and said that Soaad had left them to go to Australia. And that was that. End of story. It was like being told tomato season was over and there wouldn't be any more tomatoes. What was a twelve-year-old kid supposed to do with that information? Two years after that, Tehran was on fire. Schools were shut down, the royal family was running away, and traitors to the revolution were being hung from trees and street-lights. Instead of the classroom, Malek would spend his days watching fights break out between student factions in front of the University of Tehran on the newly coined Revolution Avenue. Until his old man, now jobless like everybody else, had come home triumphantly one after-noon and made another announcement—he had procured visas and they were going to America. They were headed to California, a town called Fresno where, according to Malek Senior's excellent contact, there was a cookie shop for sale at a huge discount. They, father and son, would start life anew in California, far from the revolution and the war. Yes indeed, they would be baking cookies in sunny California.

The bus, already hiccupping in fits and starts, finally broke down just outside of the town of Hamadan, next to a souvenir shop that sold local dolls that looked like poorer versions of Russian grandmothers. There was an eager Dutch traveler on the bus too, who kept taking pictures of the blind Iraqis. The fellow, tall and lean and very blond, made himself useful and escorted one blind Iraqi after another outside of the bus and onto the grassy area, and he never stopped taking pictures.

Children had begun to cry. An Iraqi woman was in some kind of pain and Malek heard whispers in Persian and Arabic that she would have to be taken to an emergency room right away.

He'd had enough. He walked over to the souvenir shop where several local cabbies were lounging, offered a price that couldn't be refused, and in a minute was sitting in the front of a yellow Peugeot being driven to Tehran, alone.

In California, his father's "excellent" contact had turned out to be a con artist. The cookie shop was an already-failing business on a too-quiet street in a backwater American town. It had driven his old man to the grave. And through it all, right up to now, Soaad had never figured much in the picture. If she were in Australia, she might as well be on the moon. Except that she had been here all along, in Tehran. What was he supposed to do with this piece of news?

"Go see your mother," Sina had said.

See her for what? To kiss and make up for lost time?

Dawn brought Tehran into view and Clara Vikingstad's voice with it.

He was surprised at the address she'd given him. Up in the Niavaran District, there was a more remote semi-restricted area where a lot of government types and ex-officials lived. The place had solid police presence, but it wasn't too heavy-handed. You just felt it; it wasn't an area to hang around at and take pictures for too long.

The mansion had a panoramic view of the city below it. Yet the miles of dirty haze that greeted the eyes was mostly discouraging. In the distance, lines of traffic in the main arteries of town snaked slowly to nowhere, and far to the south everything turned to a grayness that looked downright apocalyptic.

Private guards opened the door and Malek was escorted to an inordinately large reception hall. There was also the usual knickknack of new money—ugly chandeliers, gold upholstery, oversized armchairs and sofas. When Clara came down, followed by a servant who kept his eyes to the floor three steps behind her, she looked like an office woman in a Tehran notary firm. Headdresses never suited her. They took away from her fire. And Malek had never seen her wear one unless she had to in public. It was too strange. It made Malek feel like they were both on foreign territory.

They were served tea and left alone.

"Whose house?" Malek asked.

The name she gave made him stop and consider his surroundings with a new eye. It was the house of a once powerful official. The man had served in every ministry since the revolution except this last one. He might have even signed off, in the old days, on a few standard death penalty orders. So the obvious question to ask was, "Why him? Why here?"

He saw the defensiveness in Clara's eyes. One time she had written a long article for some magazine describing the lives of American soldiers in Iraq. It had been a serviceable, true-to-life piece, depicting her subjects as warriors and vulnerable and confused and basically well intentioned. Except that things were a hell of a lot more complicated than that. He'd told her that "any old hack" could write this obvious stuff. And her face had taken on the same look back then. *If a reporter doesn't write the obvious, then who will?*

She said, "Elections are next year. This guy might be back in the game. He's progressive. He advocates change."

"So you've come and put up tent at his place and become his concubine?"

She didn't show anger, but said coolly, "I ought to slap you."

"Come on, Clara! After the guy fattens his Swiss bank accounts and builds himself a few of these McMansions, he suddenly softens up, starts seeing the light, and advocates change and democracy? Is he remorseful now? He's concerned about the common people?"

She just looked at him, waiting for him to finish his short rant.

"Man's got blood on his hands," he added.

"Who doesn't have blood on their hands, Rez?"

More tea was served. Tea was always bloody well served. A country where you drank an average of fifteen teas a day, and each was more piss-weak than the last. Why couldn't the Iranians learn from the Turks how to make real tea? And now he felt like he was having just another version of the conversation he'd had with Sina about him working for QAF. *What is Clara really up to?* he asked himself. Answer: a major scoop. That's what she wanted. It wasn't enough for her to be in the select club of foreign correspondents. She wanted to report deep from the inside. She wanted a Pulitzer.

All he could say was, "You're playing a dangerous game, Clara. You know how it is here. When they decide to put you in their crosshairs, they can destroy you. Yes, even you."

And now he watched her with concern. There were things about Clara he didn't particularly like. The scope of her ambition, for instance, or the fact that she'd pretty much forgotten about him until she needed him again. But Clara herself he liked. At heart, she was a soft touch. He had seen her help others than himself. He had seen that look of utter mourning on her face more than once in Iraq. And she had courage. She was not one of those rear-door journalists. She went for the jugular and never thought of her own skin first. For all these reasons, Malek's concern for her was real. He owed it to her to protect her. This wasn't her territory. Things could go wrong. Things *did* go wrong.

She laughed off what he'd said and pushed him to drink his tea. "What's the worst that can happen to me in this place? Next year, maybe not *my* bad guy but the other bad guys win the election. And if I'm still here, maybe they decide to throw me in jail for a while. I'm an American. How long can they keep me in a cell? Three weeks? Three months? I'll come out of there a little leaner, I'll go home, and—"

"Write something about it?" Now he saw that not only did Clara not worry about being thrown in an Iranian jail, she actually counted on it. It would give her cachet. He shook his head and smiled for her. "Okay then. You're the boss. I'm just a lowly interpreter here."

"Stick with me, kid."

She'd saved him in Baghdad. Yes, she had. So why should her ambition not include this pompous house and its former minister of whatever?

She poked him, "You'll stick with me, yes? We're going to be in for quite a ride. There are things brewing here. I feel it. It's big. I haven't come back here just to bag a few reports. I'll need your assistance. I trust you. Do you have what it takes to stay next to me?"

"Clara, I have a job back in New York."

"Keep your job. Your job is good for you. But I'll need you now and then for the next year or so. I'll need you next to me. And I'll pay your airfare every time. Can you do that? Can you stay close and on call?"

He thought about Sina. And about Soaad, his mother. You couldn't remain disengaged. Not here. Things happened. Clara was a tough woman. But being tough in Tehran, that was more a liability than anything.

He said yes, he'd stay close to her. Then in Persian he added, "I am at your service, boss."

It was a small side street off Ferdowsi Square in the heart

of the city, far from where he'd met Clara that morning. Malek sat hunched on Sina's motorcycle. There was a kebab house down the street where bike messengers were busy riding in and out during noontime. He could have passed for one of them, the green vest and several days of old stubble blending him right in, making him look like a kebab delivery boy on a midday rest. When he had gone on jobs with Clara, he would usually shave and put on good clothes. It made a difference. And it made a difference from city to city too. In Tehran, the lightness of his skin and a clean suit would actually get his foot inside doors that were impossible otherwise. And next to Clara, people often took him for a Westerner with enviable native fluency. They gave him respect, called him "sir." Sometimes they wouldn't even accept that he was simply one of them, just another native. Yet that same clean look would have gotten him killed in Baghdad in 2005. You had to know when to blend in and when not to.

The thought brought him back to Sina. One day in their senior year of college, Sina had run a hand on his own brown face and told Malek, "Skin matters, brother. I'm on the outside looking in on America." Sometimes he would jokingly call Malek "His Whiteness." Other times he would go on tiresome riffs of race talk, about the iniquities the Americans had done—as if his grandparents had been born slaves in some plantation in Louisiana instead of having been one of the richest families in all of the Middle East.

It was something to consider: would Sina Vafa have ever ended up back here, doing what he did now, had his skin been three shades lighter?

Malek shook his head to get rid of the cobweb of thoughts. More water under the bridge. To each his own. All that nonsense.

At one point a small woman came out of the building. The age was right, but she looked nothing like his mother. Then again, what was Soaad supposed to look like? He remembered her as much taller than this woman. But maybe that was just a child's vantage point of thirty years ago. He watched as she walked past the kebab house and came back some minutes later carrying fresh bread. She bit into the fabric of her full black *chador* to hold it over her face and still be able to carry the bread with a free hand. Malek's mother had never worn a *chador*. She had been a schoolteacher, for God's sake. She was educated. No, that was not her. He refused to believe it.

"I spoke to her, you know," Sina had said. "She almost fainted when she found out I knew you. Said she'd seen you on Persian satellite TV giving an interview after your book came out. She'd wanted to contact you then, but didn't dare, and didn't know how."

So what next? *Hello, could you buzz me in? I happen to be your son.*

Malek kick-started the bike, took a last look at the building, then slowly rode out toward the traffic circle on the main avenue.

It was on the third day that Sina rang him. This was a good sign. It meant he wasn't operational. On *mamuriyat*, as they liked to call it in the jargon.

"Did you see your mother?"

"I went to the address you gave me." After a pause,

Malek asked, "Why is it important to you I talk to her?"

"Mothers are important, Rez."

Yes, they were. They could mess you up or break your heart or disappear and not give you an inch of love. Or they could be, if you were damn lucky, everything you ever dreamed of. It had taken baking a whole lot of cookies in a failing cookie shop, in a strange town in California, before Malek had finally managed to put her out of his mind and shut the door on that part of himself. Did he really need Sina to remind him mothers were important? It was that motherless immigrant life in America that had made both of them hard. Now that very hardness seemed questionable. Mothers were certainly important. He just didn't know if that thought meant the same thing or something entirely different to Sina.

After that quick exchange with Sina, Malek rode to an Internet café near Valiasr Square to check his e-mail. Rows of college-age kids sat in small cubicles in chat rooms, some of them obviously looking for husbands and wives abroad. The two e-mails that weren't garbage had to do with Malek's job, one from the head of the department telling him he'd been placed in a couple of committees for the upcoming year.

Malek looked around, then out the window at the mad Middle Eastern traffic outside. Out there on Valiasr Avenue you'd have to be something of a tightrope walker to be able to cross the street in one piece. Buses, decrepit old cars, brand-new expensive SUVs, and fanatical motorbike messengers and pedestrians contested every inch of space on the asphalt. The only thing missing was maybe a donkey cart and a caravan of camels. And in a few weeks he'd be leaving all this behind again to go back to committee meetings and teaching.

The other e-mail piqued his interest far more. It was from James McGreivy. The former Marine captain who was going to join his department come September. The writer of *Winter in Babylon* fame. It was a polite letter. Sure of itself and free of that chirpy enthusiasm of a lot of work-related communications with Americans. McGreivy wrote that he had taken on this teaching job to see if there was life after the military. He said that he had just finished reading Malek's book of reportage and found it interesting that the two of them had been, in a way, on opposite sides of the same battles. This of course wasn't true, but Malek didn't mind the overblown acknowledgment. The truth was that McGreivy's book was a small jewel that a lot more people should have known about. He had written of American soldierly life and his own gradual disillusionment with the war he was fighting in, especially after the Second Battle of Fallujah. And he had written about it with sensitivity and insight. It made Malek wonder why McGreivy had accepted the offer at this cash-strapped public college in Harlem rather than somewhere far more prestigious. *Why compete for my job?*

Should he answer the e-mail? He was interested in this man. And it was true what he'd told the department head about having used McGreivy's book in his own classes. On the inside jacket flap there was a photo of McGreivy looking handsome and immaculately blond, at the same time rugged and strong and fiercely intelligent. An American through and through, Malek remembered thinking. But one that was maybe a little out of date too.

He clicked *Reply* and simply wrote:

Dear James,
Greetings. I am back in the old neighborhood, Tehran to be
exact. I am sitting in an Internet cafe having just read your
gracious note. I'm sure we'll have a thousand things to talk
about back in New York. I send you my regards.
Reza Malek

Not overfriendly. But friendly enough. If the man
was going to take his job, maybe at least they could do
it without blood.

The next several days Clara needed him full-time. She
had a security detail now and Malek was not allowed to
ride in her car. So he rode with a couple of tough-looking
men in a second car instead, men who joked incessantly
about the probable color of the panties of women on the
street wearing full *hijab*. On the second day the guards
became more comfortable with Malek and included
him in their chatter. One of them even wondered out
loud why they should be following a foreign journalist
around town when there was more important work to
be done. When they both zoomed on Malek's face for
an answer, he told them the truth: "I was hoping you
gentlemen would know."

On the third day they drove all the way to Qum, a
clerical city some two hours away from the capital. "The
Man," as Malek had come to call Clara's host, had lined
up an important interview for her, a well-known opposition cleric under house arrest. But they would not
allow Malek to enter the house of the cleric to trans-

late for Clara. So he sat in the tinted Range Rover with the two guards for the next hour and a half as a human storm began to gather outside. First there was just a group of three thugs who showed up. Next there was a larger group. Voices were raised and somebody started denouncing the cleric for seeing the American journalist. Before long there were fifty or so men out there. Police came and stood watching, the whole thing a setup. The guards that Malek was sitting with did not lose their cool, though; they were used to these confrontations. But he could see they were counting the minutes and were angry that the foreign journalist had gotten them in this hairy situation. Finally, both of them jumped out of the car and, joining the driver and another guard from Clara's car, positioned themselves in front of the cleric's house.

Someone threw a rock at the cars. Then another. Soon Malek was sitting alone watching a hail of stones hitting the windshield and sides of the car. He could not get out without risking being hit on the head. It was when several boys dashed toward the car to try, futilely, to turn it on its side that things exploded. The guards ran at them with batons swinging, their sticks looking exactly like the ones police used for riot control. In the melee, Malek finally managed to slip out of the back door, but was instantly grabbed by a pair of hands that threw him against the side of the car.

It was like being on autopilot. One time in Karbala a bomb scare had set off a stampede outside a mosque. He had crouched low, his back to Sina's back, so that they had fended off the rushing bodies coming at them as if they were in a wrestling ring. It wasn't a matter of bravery, just adrenaline. And fear. Afterward, he had quietly gone somewhere and thrown up. Now he didn't feel so much fear as anger, especially anger at Clara for having gotten them into this mess. The whole interview with the cleric could have been arranged far more discretely, if she had wanted it so. But no, she had wanted *this* to happen. To make some kind of a headline. She was inside there, probably on the roof or the second floor, watching, taking pictures, while out here her bodyguards were forced to fight a crowd ten times their number.

Malek swung wildly but with force, determined to hurt and break bones. In the middle of it all he recalled Captain James McGreivy and had an irrational wish to have this man by his side. And thinking about Mc-Greivy, even as he was throwing punches, again he was taken back to Iraq. The individual heroism of a lot of these Americans had never ceased to make his jaw drop. One time he'd watched a young lieutenant jump out of a Bradley and start directing dangerously bottled-up traffic in a location everyone knew was infested with snipers. Clara had remarked back then, "Look at *gorgeous* over there! We don't make Hollywood films. Hollywood makes *us*."

The police were rushing in now. And a crowd of white-shirted, bearded men stood there, like extras in a film, waiting for some sort of cue. Malek's face was bloodied and he found himself and the rest of Clara's security detail backed against a wall while rocks resumed flying at them. He was thankful when the cops finally broke up the scuffle and began pushing people away.

Malek turned to a guard with a bad gash on the side of his face. "Are they arresting us?"

"That's why they came here." The man spat in disgust, "That's why we came here. To get arrested. Politics is shit, brother Malek. It's shit. Save yourself the trouble, go back to America."

The Man himself had apparently come down to Qum and vouched for his people, including Malek, to be let out of the police station. The next day, the more radical newspapers ran articles about "foreign elements" working to corrupt the "glorious revolution." Clara's name was mentioned alongside The Man, and pictures of the cleric's house with the crowd gathered in front of it were on display. The cleric himself was just about called an apostate and it was suggested he should be brought to trial by the Clerical Court for accepting suspicious foreigners into his home and inciting riots in the holy city.

Malek was tired. And hurting. At some point in the fracas he had received a pretty hard wallop from a stick just below his shoulder. A little farther up and he would have had a cracked bone. His new friends, the two bodyguards, had dropped him off at the central bus terminal at Argentine Square, and he had decided right there and then to catch a bus to the Caspian shore. There were people he could have looked up in the north too. But he needed to be alone and try to get his head together. The whole episode down in Qum had been one of those nasty businesses where you couldn't know who was working against whom and toward what purpose.

Two days later, when he checked his e-mail from the little motel he was staying at between two decrepit beach towns, he saw that Clara had written him. Her visa hadn't been revoked, but she'd decided it was best she leave the country for the time being. She meant to come back for the following June elections, *and I expect my favorite interpreter in the whole world to be right alongside me.*

Before answering her, he scanned the American papers online to see if there was mention of what had happened to Clara in Qum the other day. There was. Plenty of it. *American journalist briefly jailed in Iran . . .*

He wrote her: *Does using people become second nature in your line of work?*

Malek stared at what he'd written for a good long time. Then he deleted the question and discarded the reply e-mail altogether.

Another e-mail was from his student, Candace Vincent. The e-mail was in two parts. The first was a link to several pictures with captions. Candace and her kids—making breakfast for them in the morning, then dropping them off at school. The second was of her being quoted in a local Bronx newspaper about a police shooting in her neighborhood. In this last picture she had braided her reddish-purple hair and her almond eyes stared past the camera. It was almost like she was gazing back at Malek, challenging him—*There are troubles everywhere, professor. You don't have to go to the other side of the world to find this stuff.*

From the motel's small computer room by the lobby, Malek had a narrow view of the sea. The water came right up to the foundation of the motel and threatened to take it down. Wherever there was beach left, it was full of debris and garbage and remnants of old homes that had already succumbed to the water.

Water made him think of New York. Sometimes he took long walks by the Harlem River, crossing the bridge at 181st Street into the Bronx, walking alongside the kinds of housing projects Candace mentioned in her writing. He'd peek into basketball courts where teenagers, often stripped to the waist, played hard basketball and would turn around briefly to glance at him like he was some crazy white guy who had either lost his way or come slumming.

He scrolled down to the second part of the e-mail where Candace had added, *Like I feared, my kids' pops is coming around these days hassling me a bit. It's okay, I think I can take care of it all. Be proud of me, professor.*

Malek signed out. And the next time he looked up at the window for a glimpse of the sea, there was someone blocking the way.

Fani said, "You ought to be careful of the company you keep in this country, Mr. Malek."

Malek thought for a moment of telling this man, who had a habit of popping up from nowhere, to get lost. "I'm just a tourist here, Mr. Fani."

"If so, then you should be even more careful."

It was possible Fani was a desperate man, Malek concluded. The idea of just how desperate Fani might be came early to Malek as they sat in a rustic teahouse high up in the hilltops overlooking the sea. You could not work alone in this business; you had to have a team or you'd be rolled—the term they used for it at the ministry was just that, *being rolled*. Yet Fani seemed to be working alone.

Malek went straight to the point: "Let me guess, you can't get to Sina Vafa because he has some kind of protection with the people he does work for. So you keep flagging me down instead. What is it you want?"

Fani looked lost for a moment. He gazed off at the expanse of blue on the horizon stretching to the Russian shore. He twiddled absentmindedly with a Bic pen. Then, recovering, he said, "Do you see this place we're sitting at, and every square meter of land from this spot to the waterline? All this real estate used to belong to your friend's father."

Old news. The landholdings, the sports teams, the stadiums and recreation centers—it was an endless river of wealth that had been theirs before the revolution. Years ago, Malek had found out that even his own father had ultimately been just another employee of the great Mohammad Vafa and his dynasty. Malek Senior was a mere accountant in one of Vafa's chain of restaurants.

Fani said, "In the old days, when your friend and I were working together, he gave me power of attorney to try to repossess his father's confiscated properties. That power of attorney had a time limitation. I want your friend to renew our contract so I can do my work."

Power of attorney. It was like some open-sesame magic act everyone wanted to get or give around here. "You mean you and Sina were colleagues?"

"That isn't the issue now. But, all right, I was his case officer."

"And you're divulging this piece of information so easily?"

"If I lost something in telling you this, I would not tell you. Besides, I'm not in that line of work any longer."

"What is your work then, Mr. Fani?"

He was a hustler and didn't mind saying so. He was

a middleman, a fixer, a guy who kept contacts in every ministry. He greased palms on a regular basis, brought people together, and when push came to shove he would make a call to a midlevel cop or a band of thugs in Tehran's south side who would then empty a building or occupy it or burn it down. He belonged to that class of men without whom nothing could get done. About a decade after the revolution, men like him had become particularly indispensable to folks who had lost their fortunes. The exiles had begun returning and staking claims on their seized properties. But they couldn't do it alone. A fellow like Fani did the legwork and took his commission. Everybody was happy that way. Why? "Because what good is a frozen property to anyone, Mr. Malek?" This way the little men in small but key positions who worked in government offices also got paid off. They would sign the necessary release forms and receive their cuts after the business or property was sold by the original owner. It was a slimy merry-go-round of men with mock smiles. A pyramid of deceit and easy money. Malek had worked here long enough to see how the network operated. So it wasn't like Fani was telling him anything new. What he didn't know was exactly how Sina had been trying to work his way through that system.

But it was also possible that Sina didn't even care about any of this anymore. He seemed content now. He had found his niche, working with those ogres at QAF. He had always wanted to belong to something bigger than himself. Now he did.

All of which brought up the questions: Why did Sina still want to give a power of attorney? *And why to me?*

Malek observed, "It wouldn't be the first time some-one simply made up a phony power of attorney. I know of several cases myself. Why not just do it? You are con-nected. You could get away with a lot more than that. Why not make up a document that gives you the legal right to go after Sina's estate?"

"You are not wrong. Anyone can make a document out of nothing. It's kind of like you writing a book, Mr. Malek." Fani smiled, no doubt thinking he'd really nailed it with that comment. "One minute there's just a blank piece of paper and the next minute you fill in the blank and that becomes your new reality. Yes, I could do it. But the prize in question, the Vafa riches, is too big to go after illegitimately. There are other eyes on it. Power-ful people. Therefore, this particular power of attorney has to be completely legitimate. No way around that."

Iraq again. An Arab man setting himself on fire. It had been in Kirkuk. Malek and Clara had gone to the Office of Reclaims where people brought in their griev-ances about land that had been unjustly taken away from them during Saddam's time. In protest, this partic-ular man had taken all his documents to the courtyard, poured gasoline on them and himself, and lit a match. People running around screaming that somebody should put out the fire. But no one did. Malek stared transfixed as if he were watching some act of sorcery. Clara inside interviewing the new Kurdish head of the office who insisted he did not need a translator and that Arabs should go back down south where they belonged. And so Malek had stood there and watched as the man and his land claim and the power of attorney and whatever else he had on him all burned to a crisp. That evil smell you never got used to. And that courtyard full of stacked documents from the previous regime. More land claims. Some of them real, some of them not . . . And fifty minutes later, when Clara had come out of the chief's office, she still knew nothing about the act of self-immolation that had just taken place. Malek had said nothing about it either. And when they'd made love that night, she had told him to stop being so damn tender.

Fani was offering him a ride back to Tehran.

"Thanks, but I'd rather stay here another day or two. Get my head together."

"As you wish." Fani called for the bill. On his insistence they'd eaten a big stew with copious portions of rice. Malek was feeling heavy. He could sleep right here.

Fani got up. Two tables away, several loud businessmen were in a heated debate about land prices somewhere nearby. Flies buzzed in little armies around the leftover food. The smell of raw onions and sweat stuck to the nose.

"A word of advice," Fani said, peering down at Malek. "Your friend, the American, the journalist, and that business in Qum the other day . . ." He shook his head. "You are playing with fire, Mr. Malek. It means nothing to me, and I am only saying this to you as someone I don't wish to see in trouble. That foreign lady *is* trouble. And the fellow she is working with, sooner or later those in power will build a case against him."

"I have no say over what Ms. Vikingstad decides to do."

"But you went with her to Qum. I know about it."

"I teach at a university in America, Mr. Fani. I'm

here for a few weeks on my summer vacation. Then I'll go back to my safe, boring life."

"I would at the very least tell your journalist friend that she's playing the wrong side."

Malek didn't blink. "What if it is her intention to play the wrong side?"

He knew the gravity of what he'd just said. And Fani understood it too. His serious expression turned to one of slight admiration and he replied, "Your American friend plays a deeper game than I would have thought."

"Americans usually do. Except most of the time they don't even know they're playing."

Fani laughed and sat back down. "Oh, how I wish you and I could have worked together years ago. You are a man after my own heart."

"What exactly is it you want from me, Fani?"

"I want you to talk some sense to your friend. Working with QAF is not a living; quite the opposite. Take it from someone who knows. Those guys are not interested in him recovering his father's wealth. But I am. The QAF people, they only care about one thing: the end of the world."

"What if that's the only thing my friend is interested in too? What if he doesn't want to recover anything anymore?"

He could see Fani was considering this possibility for the very first time. He was frowning. He didn't like the idea that you could not talk sense to a fanatic. "I have a hard time believing that. I have a hard time believing Sina Vafa is no longer interested in getting back what is rightfully his."

"That's only because you are measuring Sina Vafa

based on your own way of viewing the world. I don't see you and me across the border right now sticking our noses into what the Americans are up to in Najaf and Karbala. No. We're sitting here eating too much food. Sina Vafa, on the other hand—"

"Do you mean to tell me he's a true believer?" Fani asked, looking genuinely intrigued.

"You were his case officer once. I imagine you know what goes on in his head as well as anyone."

Malek broke a long pause by asking Fani to drop him off at his motel. Once in the car, Malek remarked, "Nothing is without a reason."

Fani, who had become strangely silent, concurred without taking his eyes off the road. "A more certain thing was never said."

"So I'm thinking, how about yourself, Mr. Fani?"

"Me?"

"You shouldn't be chasing after someone like Sina Vafa all by yourself—no matter how much he is potentially worth. You could have stayed with, you know, your own people, former colleagues. Why did you leave the service? What happened? Was there not enough to go around in the drug-transit business from Afghanistan to Turkey? Or from the black-market ports out of the Gulf? Your former colleagues control everything in this country, not to mention southern Iraq and western Afghanistan. And, truth be told, there is just one degree of separation between them and those end-of-the-world freaks at QAF."

Fani kept his eyes on the twisting jungle road. "Yes, but sometimes that one degree of separation is everything."

"Exactly. So why not stay in the service? I imagine it might have turned out far more profitable in the long run. Did you cross one of the bosses? Is that what happened to you?"

"What I do now, Mr. Malek, is something clean. I bring back to life dead assets for people who have lost all hope of ever getting them back. In the process, I collect my fee. It is a lot different than the drug trade, a lot different than profiting from American blockades against us. In short, what I *don't* do is import baby-milk powder and hold out until the price is right. What I *don't* want is to make my fortune over hungry babies and junkies."

Nice speech. Admirable sentiments. Maybe half true. Maybe all of it lies. "But why insist on Sina Vafa? There must be a thousand cases like his."

"None is bigger than his case. I can retire after this one. Besides, Sina Vafa owes me. I got his father's confiscated house back for him. Don't look so surprised. He never told you? Ask him when he returns to town. Better yet, ask his mother."

"His mother?"

There was acid in Fani's laugh. He was recalling something and he was not happy about it. He actually stopped the car, checked his cell phone for a number, and asked Malek to enter it into his own. "Give his mother a call. You are here for now. You might as well find out a few things."

"What makes you think I'm interested in finding out?"

"Because when I was Sina Vafa's case officer, he talked a lot about you."

"What did he say?"

"He said that he trusted you unconditionally. Even though you considered yourself an American. He said you would do anything for him, and he for you. He said that the love you have for each other could make everything right. Mr. Malek," Fani's face turned serious, "do that! Make everything right."

The Sarv skyscraper complex, surrounded by a network of highways and brown hills that gave it an eerie California appearance, looked like an aging bride down on her luck. It was a row of tall buildings once fashioned for rich families like Sina's. The revolution and the ensuing confiscations of properties had left the place a ghost of its former self. Eventually, new money had moved in. New money meant conservative merchants of the Grand Bazaar of Tehran with deep ties to the Islamic Republic. Nowadays the buildings were a combination of the old money and the new, living side by side and despising one another with a venom that made the place feel decidedly malevolent.

Malek had to remind himself that he was only here for a very specific reason: his best friend, his *brother*, had gone bad, and a special kind of bad that turned everything it touched, including Malek's life, into a lie. So at some point between the taxi ride from the Caspian shore to Tehran he had decided he was going to get to the bottom of Sina's case. His friend was somewhere in Iraq right now. Doing what? Teaching some strapped and ready-to-die twelve-year-old boy how best to approach an American roadblock? There was an inconsistency here. Things should not have panned out this way, at least not for someone of Sina Vafa's background.

So if there was an answer, it was on the thirteenth floor, buzzer three of building C.

A slight, gray-haired man with moist eyes opened the door and welcomed him in. Malek was immediately surprised at how tiny the place was. He had expected Sina's mother to be living under better conditions. From the doorway, he could see a cramped living room, a single bedroom, and a tiny kitchen that was not much bigger than his own in Harlem.

Yet standing tall in front of a frayed old couch was Sina's mother, a picture of elegance dressed entirely in black, as if she were in mourning. She looked like something out of a Mughal painting, more Indian than Persian, with piercing dark eyes that held him in check for a moment so that he was not sure if he should approach her or wait to be addressed. In truth, everything here was incongruous. This woman was of another time. Semiroyalty. Malek was aware that her sixty-some years of life had seen it all—from dream homes and holidays spent in wealthy playgrounds like Monaco and Gstaad, to the revolution, and finally this, an oppressive little apartment and a second husband who in another time might have been her chauffeur.

She seemed to read much of what was on Malek's mind.

"Nobody wants to live on the thirteenth floor, Mr. Malek. Bad luck. The units on this floor used to be servants' quarters in the old days. In fact, our own servants lived here back then. When Sina returned to Tehran and threw us out of the penthouse, Afshar and I managed to scrape enough money together to buy this place. It is all we have. Forgive our appearance."

Malek turned for a second look at Afshar. The fellow had probably been some midlevel clerk thirty years ago. Purged from his job after the revolution. Thrown to the dogs. Travel a thousand miles in any direction from Tehran and you'd find plenty like him. Men who had been plugging away at their little desks until something changed, a revolution or a military coup or even a bloodless changing of the guard. And suddenly they were out of jobs, made obsolete, left dangling. For Malek, looking at Afshar was like looking at his own father and the army of aging men like him who had been waiting year in and year out to be unpurged.

He didn't know how to address Sina's mother, so he began to say, "Mrs. Afshar," but she stopped him.

"Please, call me Azar." She finally smiled and, sitting down, gestured for him to join her. "I'm surprised that you've come. I never expected to see a friend of Sina's here."

Afshar excused himself and disappeared into the kitchen.

"About the penthouse you just mentioned—" Malek began.

"I assume you know that everything Sina's father owned was taken from him. It is odd that a man like him did not have the foresight to keep at least some money out of the country. But that was him, so sure of himself. He thought Iran was his playground. And he died, so I've heard, a desperate man, without a dollar to his name in Los Angeles. But I remained behind. We were already living apart, mind you." She glanced away and seemed to try to recollect exactly when everything had gone to pieces. Malek gave her time. He felt like an accidental detective all of a sudden. None of this was really his business. Or—if he was going to agree to be Sina's legal representative in this town—maybe all of it was his business. He wanted Azar to give him something to bite on, something meaty that would suddenly explain everything that Sina had become in the past decade.

She perked up and smiled again. "Do you know, I heard about you. You wrote a book. Yes, yes. I saw you on a satellite show a couple of years back. One of those shows they beam from America. It's illegal for us to watch them, of course, but we all do."

Malek gave his thanks. At that moment, Afshar walked back into the room with tea and some sweets. After serving them, the husband went and sat in the far corner by himself, watching them, his intent rheumy eyes looking like they weren't attached to a body.

"Maybe it's that Sina partly blames me for his father's demise. Maybe he thinks it would have been different if only I had been there with them! I know Sina had a hard life in America. It's true?"

Malek nodded. "It wasn't just him. We were all exiles back then. But each of us made it somehow and it got easier after a while. Sina and I went to college together."

"So you told me over the phone. Mr. Malek, years ago when Sina called and said he was coming back to Tehran, I was beside myself with joy. At the time, even though I had no real claim on the place, I had managed to get the penthouse back for us from the revolutionary courts." She regarded her husband like some beloved piece of furniture. "What I mean is, Afshar here managed to get it back. It was a lot of work, but he did it. He did it for me and he did it for Sina. It took a long time and a lot of sweat. The courts were willing to give back one piece of confiscated property to each family. I'm sure you've heard about that law. Please drink your tea."

Malek drank. "And then he threw you out of the penthouse?"

"He did," Afshar answered from his corner. "We went from living on the top floor of this building to living in a mousetrap. What happened was one day Sina showed up with a man."

"Fani?"

"Yes," Afshar looked at Malek curiously, "that is his name. They came with some papers saying that we had no claim on the place and must leave."

"You didn't fight it?"

"Fight what, Mr. Malek?" Azar asked. "Sina was the legal inheritor of his father's estate. As his mother, I am merely extra baggage. I count for nothing. And so here we are, in the servants' quarters on the thirteenth floor where no one wants to live. I should start crying right now in front of you. But I won't. My heart has turned to stone, though not out of spite. The revolution destroyed all of us. As I'm sure in some ways it did you. It turned brother against brother, father against son, and Sina against me."

"Why him against you?"

"Oh, I don't know. Sina has decided to stay angry at the world. And Afshar and I happened to be available for him to be angry at back then. But we have not heard from him in quite some time. It's peaceful now. We are peaceful and poverty-stricken. It is better this way."

"Mr. Malek," Afshar called softly.

"Yes?"

"Why are you here?"

Malek recalled the day he'd seen his first public hanging. He must have been eleven years old back then. The revolution in full swing. In the distance a crowd had gathered below a pair of feet dangling from a yellow crane, the kind of yellow crane he had a toy replica of at the time. It had made him think of the circus for some reason. Like it wasn't real. Or it was real, but a different kind of real. Then there had been more of them. More and more hangings every day. The revolution like a grand scythe taking off heads in its wake. Until the day his old man had come home and said they were getting the hell out of this country before it was too late.

Why am I here? you ask. Because we all got a rotten deal. Like that Arab in Kirkuk who burned himself.

Malek replied, "Sina never said a word to me about his dealings with the two of you."

He watched the man and his wife. They were in tune, so much so that each knew when to take a turn speaking or remaining quiet. A tandem. Malek could well imagine what life must have been like for this woman after the revolution. She had somehow found the little fellow, her husband, and attached herself to him as you would a buoy. In time they had become life vests for each other. In the absence of better options, perhaps it was possible you could grow to love your life vest.

It was Afshar who spoke again: "Why should Sina tell you about us at all? He threw his own mother out of the house, didn't he?"

The man had kept years of being angry in check. He had spent every last dime he had toward getting that penthouse back, then Fani and Sina had just come in one day, waved a court order in their faces, and thrown them out.

"Please," Azar chipped in, "you have taken the trouble to come here. Tell us why."

He explained that it was actually Fani who had said he should visit them.

Azar and Afshar regarded one another. It was a moment of recognition. Then Azar smiled. "I see. Now my son has gone and betrayed that awful man too."

"I wouldn't call it betrayal. He simply won't give Fani power of attorney for the rest of the Vafa estate."

"Aha!" Azar suddenly switched to fluent British-accented English. "The Holy Grail, Mr. Malek. That power of attorney is like the Holy Grail in our town." She turned to her husband who hadn't understood the English and explained, "I just told Mr. Malek that power of attorney from my son is the object of everyone's desire."

The three of them sat in silence for a minute. It was as if Azar's speaking English had thrown them into a new space and they had to be careful of where they trod.

Malek broke the silence. "Sina wants to give it to me."

"*It*, Mr. Malek?" Azar said.

"The power of attorney."

Afshar popped up from his seat before realizing he was showing too much excitement and then immediately sat back down. Malek had hit a nerve and he could see it in Azar's face too. She was looking strangely at him. "Why would my son wish to give you that power, Mr. Malek?"

"I came here today to ask you that."

"Why not ask Sina himself?"

"I thought you might offer me a different point of view."

A half hour later when he was taking his leave, Malek wasn't much more enlightened than when he'd arrived. In fact, his sudden revelation to the couple had made them extra cautious with him. As if armed with a legal document from Sina, Malek would one day come here and throw them out of this apartment too. But then, just as he was about to step out, Afshar grabbed his arm and said, "Mr. Malek, if you should one day have that legal document on you and we were to ask for your help, would you oblige?"

Malek stood there a moment letting Afshar hold onto his arm. Sina's mother was hanging back, but watched with interest.

"Would I help you? It depends on the sort of help, I suppose. You have something you need help with, Mr. Afshar?"

"I might."

He felt sorry for the man. For the couple. He was in an odd position of power all of a sudden and he wanted to put the two of them at ease if he could. "You might need my help then?"

"Yes, I . . . *we* will need help with something. But," Afshar hesitated, "there might be something in it for you too."

The man was offering him a deal of some sort. It was funny and sad, in the way only a city like Tehran could make one feel. Malek gently lifted Afshar's hand off his own and, after giving it a reassuring squeeze, released it. "Just call me when that day arrives."

* * *

It was ten days and Sina still hadn't returned. Malek had gotten into the habit of drawn-out tea mornings at the Turkish place across from Sina's apartment, then hours of meditative spins on the motorbike. He had no close relatives in the city. When he so suddenly moved with his old man to California, the ties they'd had here had been severed permanently. There was Soaad, of course. But he still had to wait to make that move. Whatever business he had with Sina, and probably with Fani, he had to be sure it wouldn't endanger his own mother. It was a peculiar sense of feeling protective of someone who he wasn't even quite sure existed.

Sina was calling him on the phone.

Malek answered, "I'm standing in front of your dad's old sports center."

"Why?"

Malek wasn't really sure why and he didn't bother to answer. He'd happened to be riding up Shariati Avenue and there it was. The place looked absurd and profitable; they'd stuck some giant bowling pin, painted yellow and blue, outside of the building next to an even bigger movie poster.

He assumed Sina must be on this side of the border again and would probably be back soon. The telephone numbers he used to call Malek had changed each time.

Sina asked, "Did you see your mother?"

"I saw *yours*."

In a dead-even voice Sina answered, "We'll talk about that tomorrow," before hanging up.

Not two minutes afterward, Malek's phone buzzed again. Another new number.

"What is it?" he asked, sure it had to be Sina. When there was no answer, he spoke again: "Sina?"

"This is Soaad," the voice said, "your mother."

He had a few memories of her. Sometimes she'd take him to the bookstores across from the University of Tehran where she would meet friends from college. They were a certain type, those friends. Even as a kid he'd felt there was something off about them. They weren't like the regular grown-ups. The women hardly dressed up. In fact, they went out of their way to look utterly plain. And the men, they looked too serious. As if they were always about to do something that required intense concentration.

They'd been Communists. He figured that out later. Not much later, though. Just months after the revolution, when the Communists and the Islamists were fighting it out openly in the streets. Suddenly all those bookstore gatherings and poetry readings she'd brought him to when he was eight years old began to make sense. Before long, most of her friends would be dead or serving long prison terms. The other side had won. The country was going to be called the Islamic Republic.

He had thought about her often during the revolution. Where in Australia could she be? Would he ever hear from her again? Was there ever a time that she had truly loved him?

In California he had at last begun to forget her. Though it wasn't actually forgetting, just tucking something away and making sure it didn't pop out of the drawer too often. Soon there was high school and the accursed cookie shop he had to run with his father.

And he had new, thoroughly American concerns that had nothing to do with the Islamic Revolution. Like the Oakland A's winning the baseball pennant or the San Francisco 49ers the Super Bowl. He'd let Soaad go a little more each day until that drawer finally stayed shut. Years later, he had actually thought about making a trip to Australia and looking up the Iranians there. He was sure he'd be able to find her if he tried hard enough. But according to his father, it was Soaad who had chosen to leave. Maybe she didn't want to be found. Maybe she didn't want him to come looking for her.

And now, in her little apartment on one of these old back streets off of Ferdowsi Square, she was making him stuffed cabbage on a late-June evening. It was an odd choice of food for that season when there was usually no cabbage to be had in the entire country. Maybe she was still a Communist, he thought half seriously. One of those die-hards who'd gone for extra training next door to the Soviet Union when there was still a Soviet Union to speak of. Maybe that was where she'd learned to make stuffed cabbage.

He watched her as she cooked. Her back to him. Her elegance, he concluded, was different than Azar's, Sina's mother. Soaad looked like, and was, a sixty-year-old yoga teacher, with long white hair that sat well in a ponytail. Her body lean and erect. Her movements deliberate, almost meditative. She had the face of a woman who studied suffering as a vocation. There was intelligence in the sadness of her ample eyes. When Malek had knocked on the door and she'd opened, she had neither broken down crying like he'd expected her to, nor thrown herself wildly in his arms. She'd merely stepped forward, put her forehead to his chest, and said, "I haven't the words right now."

She had been getting by for the last twenty years with the yoga courses. Though lately she had to spend more time at home taking care of her sick neighbor. The stuffed cabbage, she'd volunteered, was as much for the neighbor as it was for the two of them.

"Were you?" he asked. She turned around from the stove, smiling and peering inquisitively at him. Malek realized he'd been so much in his own thoughts that he'd assumed she'd know what he was asking. "Were you with one of the Communist cells? I mean, back in those days when I was a kid and you took me around to places."

"That was a long time ago. It was another life. Another world."

"Why did you leave us?"

Soaad turned off the stove and came and sat across from him at the small, round kitchen table. There were no photographs in the apartment. That was what he'd noticed. Scant furniture. Not unlike Sina's place. But there were a lot of flowers. She liked flowers. He'd bring her some next time.

"Your friend Sina didn't tell you?"

"Sina just told me he had found you. That was all he said."

"What I was back then, and why I left you, they are all part of the same story. It doesn't matter, Rez."

"I disagree. I believe I'm owed an explanation. And I want to hear the explanation from your own mouth, not from Sina Vafa."

She took a deep breath. "One day two men were waiting in a car for me. I used to teach at a middle school, if you recall. They had photographs."

That had been a couple of years before the revolution. Different players. But the precision was the same. Malek knew the story by heart: They took you somewhere and were methodical about it—*All we want is for you to report to us from time to time about your acquaintances.* They wanted her to snitch on her Communist friends. She had a choice of cooperating or they'd take the photographs of her and her lover and hand them to her husband. They particularly wanted to know about *him;* they wanted her to report on her own lover.

He let her tell it to the end, though he already knew what was coming. She had come home one day and simply confessed to Malek's father. It was the only way she knew to get out of that bind.

"I could not be an informant, Reza. There are a million stories like mine in this country. Some of us chose one way, some the other. Your father took it quietly. Quiet rage, I'd say. His only stipulation for the divorce was that I disappear from your life for good. That's why the fiction about Australia."

"You could have looked me up during the revolution. Things were different then."

"I did. One day I called your father and told him we had to talk. He agreed to meet me near Café Naderi and I told him I really needed to see my son. He did not say no. All he said was that I should give him a little time so he could prepare you. Weeks passed. When I called again, a stranger answered the old telephone number. So I came by the house. There was a new superintendent in the building. He didn't know me. He was the one who told me the two of you had left for America."

She got up and started to excuse herself. She had turned chalk-white. For a second Malek thought she might pass out on him. Two and a half decades after she'd been summoned to the Intelligence Ministry, it had been his turn to be called in. Both of them had said no. They had this much in common. He reached out and grabbed her hand and told her it would be okay.

"Nothing will ever be okay." And then she finally broke down and began to cry. She was tough, though. Almost right away she recovered, looked him square in the face, and said, "I have to take food to my neighbor. You know, Anna really wants to see you. She has been saying so ever since we saw you on satellite television talking about your book."

"Why didn't you reach out then if you saw me on TV? There's the Internet, you know. The world is not so closed anymore."

"I did not know how. I mean, I did not dare, Reza *jaan*." She went to the stove and put a plate together for her neighbor. "Anna is Polish. She has lived here since World War II. I have not told her you are here. If I did, she'd drag herself from bed to see you. She is very sick. She is all I have left here."

Turned out they had come after her again. Different men this time. They'd taken her lover too, whom she'd meanwhile married. *Mr. and Mrs. Commie, Pinko, Red!* Malek thought with just a hint of spite. Nevertheless, he was trying to muster sympathy for Soaad's second husband, the man who had essentially taken her away from him. The man who they had killed. But they'd killed a lot of people back then. Did one more make a difference?

Surely. It had made a difference in Soaad's life.

Malek sat in that barren apartment and listened to the sounds of the city. He was self-conscious. *I am sitting in my maman's house now and it feels strange.* She would tell him how she'd spent that year in jail after the revolution. How she'd learned yoga in there from another inmate, and when she'd come out, she'd stuck with it. It had saved her life. Literally. She was already purged from her teaching job at school. So she began to teach yoga. It was not a bad living. There were a lot of rich folks in the city who wanted to look good and fill their time. And her husband? "I don't know why they let some of us go and killed the others. We were all godless Communists to them. I can't tell you how bad it got here for a few years. The killings. That endless war with Iraq. The cloud that fell over our lives."

Thirty minutes later, when she returned from her neighbor's apartment, he simply asked her, "Did you love him?" She looked at him quizzically. "Your second husband. Did you love him?"

"I did."

"Then why marry the old man, my father, in the first place?"

She sat back down at the table, resting her chin in both hands. "I had been in trouble since high school. Politics. My own father, your grandfather, came home one day and said there was a suitor for me. A much older man. At first I thought I'd fight it tooth and nail. But I knew I hadn't a choice. They wouldn't have allowed me to take the university exams. I figured if I married, at least I'd have to deal with just one person, a husband. Your father was a decent man. An ordinary man. He had no trouble with me taking the exams for college. He even encouraged it. Said education was the key to life. I'm so sorry, Reza *jaan*. I feel like I've been disappointing people my whole life."

"You did what you thought was right. That's not a crime."

She smiled weakly and served him a plateful of stuffed cabbages with yogurt and fresh bread. She was trying so hard. Why had Sina insisted so adamantly that he contact her? No matter. At this point he was just glad that his friend had insisted, even going to the length of giving Malek's number to Soaad and telling her to call *him*.

Soaad nudged him to eat. "And you? What did you do in California after you left here?"

"We had a cookie shop. We baked cookies. The old man, he got sick after a while. America was like *Merikh* to him, Mars. I think getting cancer was the best thing he ever did for himself over there. He sold the business at a loss. Cooped himself up in his room and read Persian poetry until he died. I don't think he bothered to learn a hundred words of English to the last day. He was like somebody abandoned on a boat somewhere."

He'd hit a nerve. She seemed like she might cry again.

Malek said, "Forget the past. But tell me this: are you in trouble?"

"What?" She seemed genuinely surprised.

"Are you in any kind of trouble here?"

"No. I . . . don't think so." Here was a woman who had been a political prisoner for one year, and whose second husband had been killed in the men's wing of that same jail—Evin Prison. So of course she couldn't be certain. Who could be certain about anything when they could come and take you away anytime they wanted to?

He stared at Soaad. "Is there anything you want to tell me? Anything at all?"

"No!"

"Before the revolution, when those men came to see you—did you agree to inform for them even once?"

Her head hung low, barely bringing the words out: "Only for three months. It was nothing, Reza. I swear, it was nothing. I told them useless things. I gave no one away. I didn't get anyone in trouble."

She looked scared. More than that, she looked ashamed. He had to put her mind at ease.

"I am not here to interrogate you. Do you understand? If you understand, nod your head."

She did.

"All right. You are not an unintelligent woman. Look at me. Look at me!" He raised her chin and caressed her cheek with the back of his hand. "You have a dossier. Even if you worked a single day for those people, you have a dossier."

"Why am I not dead then? Why did they not kill me after the revolution?"

"It was a chaotic time. You said that yourself. You were not high on anybody's list. Nobody bothered to peek into your file twice." He went silent for a while before adding, "Nobody except Sina. He found your dossier." Malek was talking more to himself now. Trying to figure out the meaning of all this.

She sat there hunched, deflated. He forced himself to finish his plate and asked her for seconds. She darted up. Happy to be doing something for him.

When she came back to the table, he asked, "Why did Sina go out of his way to find you?"

"I don't know, but I'm glad he did. Because you are here today." Her voice was almost pleading. Like she wanted to convince herself of something. "We're together at last. Isn't that what matters?"

"Yes, that's what matters," Malek offered, consoling her.

Two men were fighting. Malek stood at the ledge watching what was happening at the bottom of the stairwell in the gymnasium courtyard. There was a circle of impossibly thick-necked men down there, all of them bodybuilders, letting the fight go on without interfering. A shout had brought Malek out of Sina's apartment. It had begun with threats which soon turned into thrown fists. Now the two exhausted men wrestled clumsily on the ground while others watched. Malek was spellbound, fascinated with the impassivity of the spectators. It was a fight that had to be fought.

A tap on Malek's shoulder. His first thought was that Fani had caught him off guard again. He turned around roughly.

Sina was smiling at him. "Welcome to the neighborhood."

Malek watched Sina watching the fight indifferently for another minute, then they both started to make their way inside.

The door closed and Sina, looking disheveled, smiled again.

It was time and Malek went right ahead and did it. He took a swing, throwing Sina to the floor against the entrance door. He stood there, waiting for Sina to get himself together and fight back. When he didn't, Malek stepped in again and booted him in the thigh. "Get up!" He wanted to wipe that smirk off Sina Vafa's face forever. "Get up, you son of a bitch. I know they've trained you to kick the hell out of me. Let me see you do it."

Sina remained on the floor with his back still resting against the door, his legs splayed out, his backpack hanging from one shoulder. "I'm tired, Rez," he said, not smiling anymore. "If it's a fight you want with me, you're gonna have to wait for another day. Why don't you go downstairs and have yourself a real fight with one of those weight lifters?"

"Why did you call me to Tehran?"

"Can we discuss this over a drink?"

"No, I want to discuss it now."

Sina unzipped his backpack and brought out a bottle. "Johnnie Walker Blue. Compliments of Iraqi Kurdistan. You can't get this stuff here. I thought you'd be pleased."

A half hour later Sina had taken a shower and was walking around the apartment wrapped in a red *long*. Malek sat on the floor next to a tray that held the alcohol and two tall glasses. He had quickly swigged several shots by himself; if he felt anything, it was remorse for having lashed out. He heard the tuning of a guitar and in a minute Sina came out of the bedroom holding an acoustic. It was the strangest sight, Sina half naked with the *long* draped around his dark body playing chords to a country-and-western song.

They should have been anywhere except at this address on Orumiya Street in Tehran. Nothing made sense. Sina Vafa made the least sense of all.

Malek spoke over the music: "You found my mother's file somehow, didn't you?"

Sina shook his head, put the guitar aside, and poured himself a drink. "There's a file, yes."

"But why even bother with my mother's old file?"

Sina's neck was beginning to bruise from the punch and he kept rubbing his pummeled thigh. "Fani found it, not me. Because it was his job to do that. Those years, when you came to Tehran to work and he saw how close you and me were, he had to check your background. It was his job. So he came across your mother's old file."

"Why would *you* need a case officer in the first place?"

"Because I'm a Vafa. Don't you get it? Sometimes they just assign you somebody. And you have to accept it."

"I didn't accept it."

"But your mother did."

Silence.

"What now?" Malek asked.

"Fani kept your mother's file on him all these years for a day like this."

"And you figured if I am the executor of your estate, I can deal with Fani myself. Yes?"

Sina, looking impatient, lightly kicked the guitar away and came and sat across from Malek. "I truly am tired, Rez. I don't want to deal with the Vafa holdings, or potential holdings, or confiscated holdings, or released holdings, or anything else anymore. I'm tired of my name. I'm tired of my dead father's name. And—"

"Your mother? What about her? You return to Tehran and then you and your case officer throw her and her husband out of the house she got back from the government."

"A mistake for which I'm sorry."

"So why not tell her you're sorry?"

"It's too late."

"I see. You want me to take care of that too. You're tired, so you want Reza Malek to take care of his own mother *and* your mother."

"Who else can I ask, Rez?"

"You are using me."

"For a good deed. If you don't accept, then a fellow like Fani will eventually take it all anyway. Would you like that?"

"I can't say that I care either way."

"You don't care about your own mother?"

It was the strangest kind of blackmail Malek had ever heard of. It was cockeyed. His best friend was coercing him to take charge of a fortune confiscated by the Islamic Republic years ago—otherwise something might happen to Malek's mother, a mother Malek didn't even know he still had until a couple of weeks ago.

He could walk away from it all right now. Just get himself up. Go to the Imam Khomeini Airport. Get the hell out. Never look back.

Sina blurted, "And don't work with that American, Clara Vikingstad, anymore. She's bad news for you."

The entire town seemed to know about the fiasco in Qum. He watched Sina pour shots for both of them. The guitar lying on the floor, an anomaly from a past that may as well have never existed. Sina Vafa was the last person in the world fit to tell him what he should and should not be doing.

Malek asked, "What did you do with the house you threw your mother out of?"

"Split the money with Fani after I sold it."

"What did you do with your share of the money?"

"Spent it."

Later on, whenever he thought about it, Malek would come back to this night as the precise moment when something broke between him and Sina. It was like he was watching his friend drifting away in a boat and there was nothing he could do to stop it or reel him back in. Something was finished. But they still had to play along.

Sina raised his glass. "Brothers like always. Yes?"

Malek too raised his glass, but said nothing.

He'd been daydreaming in Soaad's kitchen. Shafts of light fell from the bamboo blind, cutting the kitchen in an almost perfect diagonal half. Outside, a street vendor was calling at the top of his voice about something to buy or sell; Malek couldn't tell which. He'd been thinking about a kebab joint in Berkeley where he and Sina would go late at night for their only real meal of the day when they were students. The portions were huge and the man behind the counter always gave them extra meat.

Earlier that day he had accompanied Soaad to a yoga workshop she'd been asked to supervise at one of those mansions in the fashionable Velenjak District, an area of expensive homes and luxury apartments in the western foothills. He had wanted to know something about Soaad's life besides that dark past, something that would lend her a reality beyond the outmoded politics and jail term and dead husbands. So he had asked to come along and then watched as she began a two-hour women's class in a bright hardwood room filled with designer yoga mats. After a while a servant politely led him out of there to an indoor pool area where the owner of the house was having a white wine breakfast party for a dozen other guests. Malek was welcomed easily into this mix, presented with a choice of wine or Bloody Mary, and then settled down as conversations took place around him in Persian, English, and French. These were the moneyed people of the city who usually held dual citizenships in Europe or North America. They went skiing a half hour away from Tehran during winter and they spent summers on the Caspian Sea waterskiing and playing cards at each other's villas. A few months of the year they visited their children in California or Europe or Canada, and they spent the rest of their time sitting by heated pools like this one, complaining about the failing Iranian currency and wishing that the Islamic regime would just be gone already.

Malek imagined his mother in the midst of all this opulence, teaching her classes for so many years and smiling at the people who basically kept her fed. He too smiled back at the easy chattiness of the rich folk by the pool and found himself feeling grateful to them. They'd saved his mother. Their money and their mansions and the private courses that only they could afford had given Soaad a space to breathe. He began to feel a quiet buzz off the drinks and mused on the presence his mother had running her class. She was respected and listened to. He'd watched her holding a particularly difficult pose for the students, momentarily glancing up to catch Malek standing by the door watching her. She'd beamed at him then, as if to say, *Now you know who I really am and what I do.*

Afterward, she declined the poolside invitation for wine, but accepted the host's offer that his chauffeur would drive them back home.

In the car she'd whispered to him, "They are not bad people, you know. They have been my bread and butter."

"I know."

"Now you have seen me teach. Do you want to see me buy groceries too? I do all these things. I really am real. Truly." She laughed.

"Yes, you are real."

It had been more than an hour since she'd gone out again for groceries. Malek waited, missing her. At last he heard the outside door turn. Soaad, holding a shopping bag, hurried into the kitchen. She set the bag on the floor and eyed Malek.

"What," he began, and then added the word that until two weeks ago would have sounded alien to him, ". . . Mother?"

He could tell she was anxious, but was keeping it mostly in check. She half turned to the kitchen door as if someone would walk in any second.

First came Fani, then behind him another man. A big, puffy-faced, unsmiling fellow who gave the kitchen a quick once-over as if he were searching for something.

Malek didn't bother to stand up. There was, he had decided, something essentially tedious about men like Fani. From the outside you would imagine their world was one of layered intrigues. But it wasn't that. It was the persistence of these guys that was their essence. They were like barking dogs that never let up.

He watched Soaad, admiring how relatively cool she

was under pressure. Even now, standing between him and these two strangers who had muscled their way into her house, she didn't allow herself to waver. She didn't break down and start cowering or invoking God and the Twelve Imams like someone else her age might have done. She just stood there, gazing back at her own son, no doubt wondering how this thing was going to play itself out. She was a veteran that way. And Malek had begun to, well, love her for it.

"You have been holding out on me, Mr. Malek," Fani said humorlessly.

In front of Malek, on the kitchen table, was an over-sized piece of paper twice folded. Malek unfolded it and let it lie on the table. It was the power of attorney that Sina had given him two days earlier. Full and complete, it gave Malek the authority to sign and sell in Sina's name anything and everything. It was one of those sealed, loophole-proof documents that people killed for. Except this particular document had a proviso written in block letters at the bottom of it, stating that it was nontransferable. It was to belong only to Malek. No third party or lawyer could make a move on Sina Vafa's behalf without Malek's direct presence. In the Islamic Republic, where these specifics mattered, it was a legal record made of steel. The piece of paper was almost holy, and it was even scribed in artificially sacred language heavy with Arabic vocabulary.

"Take a look for yourself," he said to Fani.

Fani told the shadow to stay outside. But the man didn't move. He was some type of gun for hire. Malek could tell by the way the sudden daft smile came over his face. It was the smile of a certain brand of mercenary. You almost never, for instance, saw it in the face of a British ex-soldier going private in Afghanistan or Iraq. But you saw it with some of the Americans. Not the seasoned pros working for the top foreign security companies in Baghdad, the guys who Clara would often try to chat up for those rare nuggets of information. But the ones with less skill and more mouth.

Malek would have liked to wipe the smile off the man's face. He wanted to get up and stick something into the guy. Everything his mother had been through, all the poison of thirty years, came down to this man now smiling at him like a camel's ass.

He decided to accept the risk of a severe beating and called out, "Get the gorilla out of my mother's place! He stinks like a mosque that hasn't been washed for a year."

Several minutes later, when Fani had barely managed to contain the other man and before cajoling him out of Soaad's apartment, the first thing he said to Malek was, "I didn't bring him here for show." Fani's face was pale and beads of sweat had collected on his forehead.

Soaad's samovar was making a hissing noise from lack of water. She'd excused herself to go attend to her neighbor and in her hurry had forgotten about the samovar. Malek filled the thing and put it back on the stove. "Please go ahead and examine the document," he said to Fani.

"I already did. I read the original copy at the same place you and your friend had it drawn up. Why else would I be here?"

"And?"

"It's a foolproof document. Even the court couldn't annul it. Congratulations."

"Fani, you have my mother's file from before the revolution. I want it."

"And then what happens? You sign over the power of attorney to me? Can't be done. The document says you can't transfer it. I'm afraid I'm going to have to keep you in Tehran indefinitely, Mr. Malek. Your signatures will be necessary for everything I work on for the Vafa estate."

"What makes you think I'll work with you? If Sina Vafa had wanted this, he would have given you the contract himself."

"Sina Vafa is a maniac. A zealot. And now that he's with QAF, he can't sign for anything and not look bad in their eyes. The only thing left for him to do was sign his entire will over to someone else. That someone else has turned out to be you, Mr. Malek."

"I can't stay in Tehran."

"Then we have a problem."

"I want my mother out of this country."

This brought loud laughter from Fani. "You want to leave and you want your mother to leave with you. What does this leave *me* with, Malek?"

They were at an impasse and remained silent for a minute, both of them hovering next to Soaad's stove without making a move to sit down. Malek finally asked, "So who is that ape you brought with you today?"

"That man is the type of guy the Americans will hire right away when they return. He'll put on a tie, shave his beard, learn a few phrases in English, and be the first in line to do security work for the Americans. Indeed, Mr. Malek, I did time in Iraq too. You weren't the only one. I saw what the Americans did."

"And what about you, Mr. Fani? What will you do when the Americans come?"

Fani's face lit up. He was glad again for their banter. "I will do very much the same. Do you know why? Because I'm the best friend you Americans are ever going to have here. I'm a man with no ideology. And I'm a lot smarter and more educated than that beast out there."

"But who is that beast? I know you didn't bring him here just to scare me. I'm already scared."

Fani took a beat too long to answer. "He's a guy who does my errands now and then."

The answer was preposterous. Malek had seen the worry on Fani's face when he'd had to pretty much beg the other man to stand outside for a few minutes. That was no errand boy out there. Probably Malek's former associates in the ministry had gotten word that he was aiming for the Vafa estates and they wanted in on it. So there was a hierarchy now. A food chain that no longer ended with a jack-of-all-trades like Fani; rather, it ended with other men, far more shadowy, devout godfathers who wanted their cut because that was their job. Between last week and this week Fani was no longer working alone; he had to answer to these other men and pay *tax*. It was a simple, well-worn structure, Malek realized; they let you move the ball up the field on your own, but when it was time to score they stepped in and said, *Salaam*, "We're in." It was, in a way, the quintessence of gangsterism.

Malek swallowed hard and proposed his deal. He would go with Fani to the places they had to go to and sign the things he had to sign, but then he would have to return to the States because of his job. He could come back again for a month during his winter break.

"Think big, Malek! When you take your cut of the Vafa estate, you will never have to work again."

He'd never thought of it that way. But of course it was true; if everybody took a cut, why couldn't he? Without him nothing would take place. He could charge his own commission. The corruption came bit by bit. One morning you woke up and you were part of that food chain.

"You yourself said this estate has a lot of eyes on it," Malek said. "It could take forever. I can't sit here until then and do nothing."

"That's fair. I also imagine you miss your beautiful city. Too bad about the towers in New York. But you Americans, you will build again. You always build. You always win."

"I'm not American."

"Oh please, Mr. Malek. You carry their passport. I envy you that. And when you guys finally arrive, I can tell everybody that I have an American friend and his name is Reza Malek. My life will remain legitimate."

Fani suddenly reached out and gave Malek an energetic handshake. Then he started to walk toward the kitchen door. Malek called him and he turned.

"What about my mother?"

Fani winked. "She's my collateral, isn't she? She stays. She doesn't go anywhere."

"Is this what the men you work for want?"

Fani gave a long look at Malek and walked out.

A man and two older women stood at a row of graves in a remote section of the cemetery.

Soaad bent down and tried to read the name on the

marker. Under a small Star of David, the name *Orba* and beneath it *Ryfka* had been etched into the stone. Then the dates when the child had lived, *1937–1942*.

Anna, Soaad's Polish neighbor, leaned heavily on Malek's arms. She could barely stand. From the pictures Malek had seen in her apartment, she had been a woman of substantial proportions in her middle years. She was wasting away now. Strands of her short white hair jutted beyond her awkwardly pasted headdress and gave her haggard face the appearance of a tail growing out of her forehead. Her eyes were sunken and hollow. She was looking beyond the rows of tombstones to an unspecified place west of the cemetery where a park named Martyrs of Islam was located. Her knees buckled, so that Malek had to cautiously wrap one of her arms around his own neck and lift her up. When they'd gotten here, there had been a hint of life in those legs. Now even that little bit was gone.

Yet it was at her insistence that they had come to the Jewish cemetery of Tehran.

Malek saw that the gaunt, redheaded caretaker of the place was still looking oddly at them from a distance. At first he hadn't wanted to let them inside, saying that the cemetery was only for Jews—even though he himself, he emphasized, was not a Jew. There had been some back and forth until Malek handed him the equivalent of two weeks' worth of wages and the man opened the door.

Meanwhile, the private car they'd hired for the day waited for them outside.

It was a well-kept cemetery, but inside the dusty old synagogue time seemed to have drawn itself to a close. Photos of former dignitaries of the community lined a couple of glass cabinets, and old tomes were scattered haphazardly on wooden benches and piled in precarious columns in corners.

It had been hard to get Anna through the place, especially since the section devoted to the Polish Jews of World War II was at the very end of the grounds. All that the sign said at its entrance was: *Lahestaniha*. Poles. Before they got to it, they had to sit for a long time on one of the benches in the synagogue so Anna could catch her breath. At one point her gaze fell on the eastern wall and on a glass case where a tanned parchment was laid out. Anna had smiled, her head drooped, and she seemed to fall asleep for a while.

Now Soaad was moving between the several rows of graves, reading the names aloud to herself, trying to digest whatever it was that had brought them here. When she glanced up at Malek, who was still holding Anna up, there was wonder in her eyes.

Walking back toward them, she called, "A lot of them were children."

Anna, her voice barely audible now, repeated, "Children. The ones who didn't get there."

"Get where?" Malek asked.

"Eretz Yisrael."

Soaad lifted Anna's other arm. "We go now, Anna. That is all right with you?"

"One more minute," she pleaded.

And so they stood there for another minute in the Polish section of the Jewish cemetery of Tehran, next to a park called Martyrs of Islam. The absurdity of it all—and the withered beauty of the scene with the three of them there—did not escape Malek. It was like he had entered another world, one that was neither Tehran nor New York, but something of another time and space altogether. He only wished there was someone he could call and share this moment with. He had not even brought a camera.

He whispered to Soaad, then mother and son heaved in unison and slowly began to drag Anna back to the cemetery gate and the waiting car outside.

For the next couple of weeks Fani's shadow disappeared. So Malek's time was now mostly spent driving from office to office with Fani alone and being introduced to this and that *hajj aqa*—men in various states of corpulence who would nod and shake hands and make no promises. It was a round of introductions at the courts and the different revolutionary foundations. The foundations were basically rackets where the confiscated estates of the previous regime were held in some kind of perpetual escrow so that anyone associated with the foundation could steal from the common trough—the Foundation for the Needy, the Foundation for the Martyrs of War, the Foundation for Martyrs' Families and Orphans. The list was endless, and so were the riches to be had. The trick was that for those who wanted to steal more than just their allotted share, each estate would have to be "freed" from the foundation's clutches. That was where Malek's power of attorney came in. If, for instance, just the Vafa Sport Center was freed, in one swoop the men who had done the freeing would have over a hundred million dollars to share amongst themselves. The stakes were immense.

And since this was how the game worked, Fani

wanted it to be known there was a *vakil*, a proxy, actively representing the putative Vafa estate. And that the rep, Malek, was in turn being represented by Fani. Each *hajj aqa* would examine the legal document, clear his throat, and offer his noncommittal "no problem," and they'd move on to the next guy. Once a critical mass of no problems was reached, Fani would begin his dance. But that was in the future and Malek's summer of 2008 in Tehran was fast drawing to a close.

One day, outside of the Central Revolutionary Court, as Malek and Fani were walking away from the building, Sina called out to them. It was the first time that Malek had seen Sina and Fani in the same place. He watched as the two former associates eyed each other, wary and familiar and cold.

"You two are getting along well, it looks like," Sina observed. He sat on his motorcycle and did not make a move to get off and shake hands. "I feel like an extra now. Not needed anymore."

"You wanted this," Malek said impatiently. "You set it up." He wasn't used to speaking Persian to Sina and the words seemed to leave his mouth somewhat warped.

Fani said something but in the din of midday traffic it was lost. Just then a yellow bus filled with kids sticking their heads out drove past, the children screaming and wearing black bandannas that had *Army of the Messiah* written on them. It was all a mad carnival where Malek felt more like a hostage than a player.

When the noise subsided a little, Fani repeated, "Aqa Sina, your friend is pulling his weight. He is all right. You stick to your own people and I'll look out for Mr. Malek here."

"But it's my name being spread around over there." Sina pointed to the court. "Maybe I have something to say about that."

"If you did, you would have said it by now," Fani countered. "What do you want?"

"Nothing. I just came to pick up my friend. There's a game on today at the stadium."

"All right then!" Fani nodded and began to retreat. Within seconds he had disappeared into the crowd.

Malek had been gauging the icy look in Sina's eyes during the encounter. "You could kill that man, couldn't you?" he asked, switching back to English.

"It would not be beneficial."

"To whom would it not be beneficial?"

"All of us."

"So what do you want?"

"Hop on. It'll be a good game."

"Your father's old soccer team?"

"The one and only. Come."

It was just a warm-up preseason game before the real season began the following month. Nevertheless, the stadium was full and Sina's team scored a couple of quick goals before settling into a comfortable defensive position for the duration.

The whole time Malek's focus remained on Sina, who watched the game with the intensity of someone who had a stake in it. Some hours later, Malek brought up the subject. "You really care if your old team wins or loses, don't you?"

They had ridden out from the stadium in a convoy of flag-waving, horns-blaring bikers heading to Razi Park in a southern district full of motorcycle mechanics.

Sina chipped in some money with a loud group of men to get *chelo-kebab*, and when the food arrived, they all sprawled on the grass near the man-made pond and began digging in with hands and plastic spoons.

Slowly, the night turned into a riot of vows about how the championship was going to be theirs this year. Men danced. Police arrived. But these were tough, bike-riding soccer fans and they were soon forcing the police to eat with them or stand aside.

Malek ate and watched Sina do the same and knew that all that his friend had ever wanted was exactly this, to simply be one of the boys. Around one o'clock in the morning, when the riders began drifting away, Sina finally answered Malek's question. "Of course I care about my old team. A man has to stay loyal to some things." He glanced at Malek. "Like you and me, for example. We're loyal to each other, no?"

They were still sitting on the grass. Alone now. A park worker sauntered over telling them they had to leave soon. They didn't pay the man any attention and he went away. In the distance, on the other side of the little pond, families lingered with their kids. On summer nights like this they stayed out till the wee hours of the morning.

Soaad would be waiting up for him right now, worried. His own mother! It was Malek's first experience of actually living with a woman, even just for a few days. She had begged him to collect his stuff from Sina's house and move in with her while he remained in Tehran, and he'd said yes. She cooked for him every night. In return, besides the daily rounds he made with Fani to the courts, he didn't stray far from Soaad and her neighbor, Anna.

"I'm going to ask you one more time: what do you do for QAF?"

"QAF doesn't exist."

"Maybe not. But what do you do for them?"

"I translate when they need a translator."

"Is there an office you go to? Do you have a desk? Do you report to a superior?"

Sina smiled. "What difference does it make? Let's say I have a nine-to-five job at a place called QAF Headquarters, does that satisfy you?"

"I'm only trying to understand."

"You've been trying to understand for many years, Rez. That's why you kept going to school. You're the guy who needed to understand and I'm the guy who had to . . ."

"What?"

"Do things. To actually live. There's a difference between living in the world and going to school, Rez."

"What you call *doing* is doing without thinking."

"Not true. I gave everything a lot of thought."

"Like deciding to tell me about my mother? Maybe I didn't have to know about her. I lived all this time without knowing."

"Is that really what you would have wanted?"

No. It wasn't what he would have wanted at all. Now he gave up trying to make sense of any of this and simply said, "Tell me anything you want to tell me. Anything!"

Sina gave him a rare serious look. "I'm in too deep, Rez. Way too deep."

"So come back stateside with me. Forget all this."

"Can't be done."

"You've committed yourself that much?"

Sina nodded. "I just want one thing from you: if you succeed with Fani, promise me you'll take care of my mother too."

"You want to make amends with her after throwing her out of that house?"

"I do."

"So go apologize. Tell her you love her."

"Not possible. Some borders you cross, you can't go back to."

There was truth to that. And it felt like Malek had to give some sort of promise to Sina to keep him from falling off the edge of the world. He said, "I'll do this whole power of attorney thing. I'll finish it. I'm doing it for my mother. And I'm doing it for your mother. Understand?"

"Thank you."

"But you," he held Sina's hand, "you know they won't even wash your body when they're done with you. They'll just throw you in some unmarked grave."

"Is there really a difference when we're gone? You really prefer a marked grave rather than an unmarked one, Rez? Is that what's important?"

When Malek told Soaad and Anna he was leaving in two days to go back to America, Anna began weeping. Soaad just stared at the wall. They were in Anna's bedroom where the smell of sickness was heavy. It was some kind of cancer. Malek didn't remember which, only that it was terminal. Maybe Anna had weeks or months. She'd already lived her life, she kept repeating.

"Please, have them bury me at the Polish section in the Jewish cemetery."

It was going to be impossible. She had nothing to prove she was a Jew. Her story had come out in truncated bits and pieces in recent weeks, whenever she could sustain talking more than a sentence or two. The cemetery trip they had taken together had really knocked the wind out of her. That night Soaad had had to rush her neighbor to the emergency room while Malek was out. By the time Anna returned three days later, there was not much of her left.

Yet Anna had taken to calling Malek "Son of Soaad." Now, using that epithet, she asked softly while lying in bed, "Why do your eyes tell me that my request will not be met?"

He explained that he'd already gotten in touch with what remained of the Jewish community of the city. They were reluctant. More than reluctant. Theirs was a close-knit community. And to be simply told there was an old Polish woman—who had been living in Tehran as a Catholic for six and a half decades—declaring suddenly that she was Jewish just didn't cut it for them. They needed strong proof, especially from other Jews who could vouch for her. On the phone they had sounded scared and eager to get off. While they didn't come right out and say it, they wanted to avoid trouble with the authorities. It was in the air. They'd been through enough since the revolution and they didn't want to give any cause for problems.

"What if I leave them my apartment?" Anna asked hopefully. "They could sell it. Use some of the proceeds for a grave for me." She had run out of steam and her eyes began to close.

Soaad stood still on the other side of the bed, observing her friend of more than twenty years. Finally she asked Malek, "Is there nothing you can do for her?"

Anna's eyes popped open and she half smiled. "Yes, do that please, Son of Soaad. Tell my story."

He saw that she had reached over and was holding out an envelope for him. The veins on her hand resembled faded ink blots. He knew so little about her. There was a picture of her on the mantelpiece with her husband, a local, who had died a long time ago. No children. Just the two of them. The man a small dark fellow, and Anna looking several dozen pounds heavier than she was now. Anna in a red dress staring at the camera some twenty-five years ago. Her secret locked in her breast, so that there was nothing to do about it but to fatten the space around that secret and throw away the key.

Malek took the envelope and peered questioningly at Anna.

"I have been dictating to your mother," she said. "It is my life story. Only a few pages. Maybe you make something of it. Some of it you already know. Don't forget me, Son of Soaad."

He pocketed the envelope. He was tired all of a sudden and felt burdened with the weight of too many people's secrets. He kissed Anna on the forehead and bade her goodbye.

Back in Soaad's apartment, she asked him when he was going to return to Tehran.

"Winter."

"Why did you find me?"

It wasn't necessarily an odd question, it was just a little late to ask it. He looked at her and didn't quite know what to say. "You already know the story. My friend Sina directed me to you."

"But you didn't have to come, Reza."

"I did. Just like I had to take that letter from Anna right now."

"I'm an act of kindness for you then?"

"You're my mother."

"What happens now?"

"I try to get you out of this country."

"I don't even have a passport. They won't issue me one. Believe it or not, I am still considered a danger to the Islamic Republic."

"It can be arranged."

"And that man who came in here?"

"Fani? I have no choice but to work with him."

"Why not just refuse?"

"I have already put my signature on documents. And men like that, you don't back out on them. It's not done. Also, he's not working alone anymore. There are others involved. Others I'll never get to see. But they're there. They smell money and they are born."

"All this is because of your friend's family, their confiscated estates?"

Malek nodded. He remembered years back when he'd taken Sina to Fresno to see his father. By then the old man was already pretty sick. And yet he had gotten on his knees and kissed Sina's—his ex-boss's son's—hands. It was the most excited that Malek had ever seen his own father, dropping down like that and putting Sina's hands to his lips. Maybe he'd thought by doing that he would somehow rewind time and they'd all be back in Tehran again—before the revolution, when everything was fine and in its rightful place, the world ticking away handsomely without the troublesome Islamic Republic, without the killings and executions, without the war and everything that followed it.

He told Soaad about that episode now.

She was silent a moment, then murmured, "It is my fault. I got you into this. You should have never come to Tehran. Forgive me."

"Listen, this business that I have with Fani and Sina, it started long before you."

"No. It started thirty-five years ago when I began informing on my friends. That is why you are having to do what you are doing now."

"You never informed on anyone. Don't forget that. And when we're finished here, your case will be closed forever. Do you understand?"

But she had already turned back to her kitchen stove and would not look at him.

Fani said to him, "Mr. Malek, do you ever watch these videos they have on the Internet?"

"I have to be at the airport in four hours. Just tell me what I want to know."

"In return for what?"

"We're either working together or we aren't. I'm signing on behalf of Sina Vafa. I need to know what kind of a man I'm signing for."

"And once you find out?"

Malek shrugged. "You have my mother's dossier. So I'm not walking away from you. I can't walk away from Sina Vafa, either. He's—"

"Your brother? At least you love him like one."

"I stick to my people."

"Who are your people, Mr. Malek? America or us?"

Malek was silent. Fani wasn't playing with him. What Fani wanted was to be sure the bird wouldn't fly the coop. He wanted assurance.

The place was in the same affluent neighborhood where Soaad had taught her yoga class. It was on a street with some European embassy at the end of the block with young Iranian soldiers posted in front. Malek was surprised that Fani had brought him here. Surely this wasn't his house. It didn't look lived in. More like a setup, a façade for a house. Books neatly stacked in a library shelf next to a window with a gorgeous view of the mountains. A spotless glass dinner table and leather chairs. Throw rugs. A few ordinary paintings and calligraphy on the walls.

And a computer.

Fani had turned it on. He went online through a proxy portal to bypass the government censors.

For the next hour Malek sat there watching one video after another on Fani's screen. They were mostly clips of contract workers in Iraq, with inflated titles like *Sniper Kills 50 Insurgents*, or more bland ones like *PSDs in Action*. After a while it resembled a video game. American private military contractors recording footage of themselves in fast-moving cars while popping off gun rounds. Some of the videos were compilations glorifying the military life, with heavy-metal music playing in the background. Malek was hooked. It put him back in a place he hadn't been to for a while. He felt the adrenaline. And soon he forgot why he was even sitting there watching all this.

At last he slowly reached over and pressed pause. His mind blank. It was like someone had hammered him on the head or suffocated him under a pillow. It took him a moment to find his voice. Fani was standing by the window gazing at the mountains.

"So?" Malek murmured.

"It may not look like it right now, but that war next door, it's winding down."

"Why did I just sit here watching this stuff?"

"It was the kind of videos found on your friend's computer."

"Why show them to me?"

"You figure it out, Malek. You wanted to know; I showed you. I have nothing to gain by deceiving you. We work together. Like I used to do with Sina. And what you and I do is, according to the laws of this land, completely legitimate. However, it would no longer be legitimate if your friend gets himself killed. Because then that piece of paper you've been carrying around with you would be worthless. As would all our efforts."

"You want to keep Sina Vafa alive."

"So do you, I assume. Though each of us has his own reasons. Talk to him. Tell him to get off Satan's donkey, as the saying goes, and stop doing the things he does across the border."

"I very much doubt that my friend is a mastermind who targets American private contractors in Iraq."

"Why? Because he's too *nice* to do that kind of thing?"

Malek had no answer to that.

"As I said," Fani went on, "that war is slowly, very slowly, drawing to a close. In the end, the men who will be left to fight are fools like the ones you saw on those videos, and people like your friend who want to do something about those fools."

"Maybe he just has a thing for violent Internet videos."

"Sure, Malek. Sure! And now I take you to the airport. It's time."

JAMES

It was brotherly love, he thought without much irony. And it was the kind of protection you wanted to give a younger sibling, even though James McGreivy, a hardened Marine veteran of Iraq and Afghanistan, was not exactly the sort of man who needed anyone's protection.

Malek hung in the back of the auditorium watching as the panel discussion turned from tensely polite to pointedly hostile. James was up there on stage taking the hits. To each side of him there were other men who had also written books about their experiences of the war. They weren't necessarily gung-ho types. But they had a special bone to pick with James. And the mixed audience could have gone either way.

The auditorium went quiet all of a sudden, panelists and the audience waiting for James McGreivy to answer a question about the Second Battle of Fallujah, of which he'd been a part. James searched the audience until his eyes locked onto Malek's. *Help me out here*, he seemed to say.

Just a week earlier, driving two hours into Long Island to visit James's mother and sick father, there had been a similar moment at the dining table. James's mother, a woman with frail milky skin and tired blue eyes that followed the movements of her eldest son around the house like she was still looking after her four-year-old, had made pot roast and some unlikely spicy cabbage that she claimed she'd learned how to cook when James Senior, a career Army officer, had been stationed in Korea. The awkwardness between the visitors and James Senior lay thick and none of the fluttering back and forth from the kitchen on James's mother's part eased the strangeness. James's father simply refused to say one word. He would not talk, period. It was bad enough that his one child who had followed his military path had written an antiwar book while the battle was still on. It was another for him to bring Malek to their house and announce, "Mom, this is my Iranian colleague that I told you about."

Malek had sat there with the pot roast stuck in his throat feeling like a bona fide alien. McGreivy Senior— looking disused, a retired colonel and former helicopter pilot with his own tours of duty from 'Nam long behind him, and with no uncertainty about who was friend and who was foe, and that if not Communists, then softness and liberal mumbo jumbo had turned his stout America to mush—was a man who had seen two of his three kids fall into every crack that this failing world proposed. His younger son, after several brushes with the law for drug possession and a felony charge, had finally put as much distance as he could between himself and the old warrior, living in some godforsaken town in Nevada where he rode his pride and joy, a Harley, and intermittently bagged groceries for a living. While the little sister had relegated herself to trailer-park America somewhere in the Midwest where she wasted away alongside a skeletal husband with a ferocious methamphetamine habit.

In the three months since the start of the academic

year, these were the sorts of details Malek had learned about McGreivy's life from McGreivy himself. And now, in this house in Long Island where America seemed set to clobber itself, father and son had sat staring at each other as if one was an unreconstructed gook killer and the other a lover of every *hajji* that ever strapped a bomb to himself and tried to kill a few Americans. What had gone wrong? Captain McGreivy, who had seemingly done everything right, who had passed the brutal Marine Officer Candidates School, and not only done well but was on the road to surpassing his father's military distinctions in every way imaginable, had suddenly upped one day and called it quits. Not only quits, but then this book he had written. This fucking book that called everything into question. Including the heroic Battles of Fallujah. What was the colonel to do with this? This son who had been the apple of his eye, his point of pride, the one bright shining kid that had kept him ticking while the two others went to hell and disappeared from his life altogether. The colonel sat home and got sick and received calls from salty old buddies in places like San Diego and Fort Bragg who asked him point-blank, *What does your son mean? Why is he writing this stuff? I thought you said it would be an excellent book about the war.*

The silence at that table. It stunk of betrayal. And sitting there, Malek had a vision of Sina Vafa in Iraq at that very moment . . . doing what? And to whom? And for what? McGreivy Senior was right; he had a point. Malek shouldn't have been in that house. His presence threw every arrangement the old man had with himself into question. Why do this to any man? Malek resented having been brought there. Even if it was brotherly love.

Even if it was some bullshit piece of fiction about how we are all people of one planet and should learn to get along. McGreivy Senior didn't want to get along. And he had earned the right not to.

And so, back in the auditorium with James McGreivy on stage, Malek wanted to shout across that audience to him, *My friend, you've taken a piss on your own people and I don't know how to tell you to fix it.*

Immediately to James's right sat a former Army Ranger who had done quite well for himself with those think tanks in Washington. Mr. Security! No doubt he could give a four-hour lecture on how to deal with terrorists and low-level wars and insurgencies, and in a few years go on to set himself up for public office. To James's left there was another former Marine who had also been at Fallujah. He had posed the question to McGreivy, bluntly, "What do you mean that Fallujah was hardly Iwo Jima? What's the point of that statement? That's an insult to every Marine who gave his life for this country."

Malek saw a cloud finally pass over James McGreivy's eyes. He could feel it coming; James was going to throw every caution to the wind. He'd had enough of this. Enough of his book and the war and these panels which he'd been sitting on for the past year to supposedly promote his book. Two words came out of his mouth, and he said it just low enough that a lot of people weren't sure they'd heard right: "Fuck it!"

Someone in the front row asked him to repeat himself.

"I said FUCK IT. No, Fallujah wasn't Iwo Jima for us, and it wasn't Normandy for them," he emphasized, pointing to the Ranger. "Fallujah was bullshit. We took a town of a few thousand half-starved Iraqis and squashed them with everything in our arsenal. It was like taking a baseball bat to a cornered lab mouse, to a mosquito. And then . . ."

This was horrible to watch. McGreivy had lost it, and because he had lost it he was exaggerating. Malek watched James as he spat with anger, his eyes meeting no one now. There were already murmurs in the crowd. And then James just bolted up and blitzed past that red-line he had already crossed: "And afterward, what did we do? We patted ourselves on the back and gave ourselves medals and called it one heck of a fight. Medals? It was those poor surrounded bastards in that two-cent town who deserved the medals. They weren't the ones with the Abrams tanks on their side, were they? Bravery? Honor?"

James's voice finally got drowned out in a sea of jeers, then a loud, clear voice from the audience called out what was probably on everyone's tongue just then: "You're a disgrace to every soldier that ever served under you."

Unable to watch anymore, Malek backed out of the auditorium to wait for McGreivy outside. Even if a fraction of what James threw at these people was true, there were still things that simply couldn't be said the way he had just said them. Least of all by Captain James McGreivy of the United States Marines. There was something untenable about this.

So Malek stood in the parking lot on a chilly mid-November evening in Arlington, Virginia, and waited. That morning he had received a call from Sina's mother, begging him to come back to Tehran even if only for two days. She and her husband needed him. He had promised them he'd come as soon as the fall semester was over.

Malek gave it another week before he asked James about Fallujah. "You don't really believe what you said down there in Arlington, do you?"

"The Corps fought a good fight in that shithole town in Iraq. No one could have done it better than us. No one ever does."

"So why did you say what you said?"

"I was tired, Rez."

James avoided Malek's eyes. They were sitting in James's office, which was still mostly bare. The college had given him a room on the other end of the building from Malek's. Piles of books sat in neat rows on the ground. Unlike most of the other offices, there were no posters on the walls. They'd also promised James a new paint job and carpeting. After two months of waiting, he had bought paint, brushes, carpet, and glue, and did the whole room in two days on his own. Malek had seen how James's relationship with the college had turned sour from day one. Everywhere he turned, the former Marine officer saw inefficiency and waste. The cloaked indolence of a run-of-the-mill public university, which Malek was used to from years of having been a graduate student, just plain maddened James. In a way, James McGreivy may as well have come from another planet. A place where only skill and ability bumped you up. He was a fish out of water here. Didn't know how to play with words, and didn't want to. He just wanted to get the job done. When he fumed, he would tell Malek, *A man's either good to go, or he's not*. And as early as the second faculty meeting of the semester he had blurted to their colleagues, "Is no one responsible for nothing? The way things are run here, it's like you're sending soldiers to war without guns and ammo."

Malek realized that his own job was safe. James would not be rehired next year. The roomful of tired old professors had gone silent, the way the auditorium in Arlington would go silent a month later. But then the head of the department, who had hired James in the first place, answered, "That's a double negative you just used, James. *No one responsible for nothing*. I thought you had better command of English, being a part of an English department, after all."

"It was said for emphasis."

"But the English language does not work that way. And by the way, up here we're not at war, in case you imagined we were. We don't train soldiers here or give them guns and ammunition."

They'd laughed at him then, a cold, academic laughter that only knew the world through the *New York Times*. Yet James McGreivy had taken that derision with a lot more composure than he would the jeers in Arlington. His healthy, boyish good looks, with those intense, narrow warrior's eyes, stood in stark contrast to the pallid bearings of the professors. He didn't worry about the next book he was going to write. He wasn't after a promotion. If he was, Malek knew, he would have simply stayed in the service. He was just an idealist jarhead, almost a decade Malek's junior, who—even after Iraq, or maybe especially after Iraq—was still seeking the damned truth. And he wouldn't shut up. Couldn't. Keeping quiet was not why he had accepted the offer of this job. It was not why he had written his book.

Which was why his students loved him. Worshipped him, more like it. James McGreivy, the idealist, had taken on the job in this inner-city college in Harlem to change the world. In the Marines he had seen for himself how you could turn just about anybody around and give them new life. He was convinced that this place was shortchanging *his* kids. He talked about the students like they were a part of his own brigade, company, platoon. He felt protective of them, told them they could do anything, and then went ahead and showed them they could do anything. One month into his teaching gig, a female student had confided to him that she'd nearly been raped. Within days, James McGreivy had gone down to the school gym and applied for a time slot to teach basic self-defense to anyone who was interested. Word had gotten around—Professor McGreivy was teaching you twenty-two moves that would save your life in any given situation. All you needed were these twenty-two moves and you wouldn't have to be afraid of anyone ever again. The self-defense class was exploding, especially with female students who flocked to him like some kind of savior.

But that was still not enough for James. Soon he was arguing with the administrators. He demanded to know why the class sizes were so large. And why was the college gorging itself on the sweat of taxpayers, holding parties at expensive restaurants for its higher staff all the time?

In other words, James McGreivy was on many shit-lists. But why should he care about that? Publishing the book had released a flood. Now he was out to fix his whole country. And if his own father thought he was crazy, or a traitor, then so be it. He'd lost a brother and a sister to the sickness that had become America. The sickness of greed, he told Malek. Greed and selfishness. "Do you know the first thing you learn as a Marine? It's to not be selfish. Because selfishness will get you and your buddies killed. You won't even survive boot camp without learning to work with others."

Malek mostly just listened. On the other side of the world, Sina Vafa was out to kill Americans because he thought they were greedy. And here James McGreivy was trying to save them because of the same thing. Reza Malek listened and wished for the soft whispers of a woman. The last woman in his life had been Clara Vikingstad, and that had been nothing but hardball, covering war and Middle Eastern politics with bouts of even harder, colder, mostly graceless lovemaking in between.

"Why are you looking at me like that?" James asked.

They'd sat silently in his office, and at some point, knowing that James kept a bottle of whiskey under his desk, Malek reached for it and began drinking. James pretended to be rifling through some papers and didn't fully meet Malek's gaze. They both taught evening classes and James still didn't have a place in the city, so he'd have to drive way out to Long Island to stay with his parents. On the nights they drank heavily after teaching, he'd just crash at Malek's place up the street and drive back home in the morning.

Malek, already feeling a buzz, said, "I think I saw you in Baghdad once, directing traffic or something."

James laughed and glanced up. "Wouldn't have been me. I had tougher shit to deal with than fucking Baghdad."

"And you know what? I think you're still trying to direct traffic. It's what you do. You can't help it. Except, you know, out here there's rules and traffic lights. It's not like it was in Baghdad. You don't have to direct traffic anymore, Captain McGreivy."

"What's with this dispensing advice?"

"You already know they won't rehire you next year."

"I know it. I don't care."

"What do you care about then? You got a girlfriend? No, you don't."

"Neither do you. We're screwed that way. No good to anyone. Especially women. But I get plenty of fan e-mail. Peace-loving, antiwar women with exquisite names like Piper and Kiara and Penelope telling me how they'd love to take a round-the-world trip with me."

"So go with one of them. Pick a tall one. Someone closer to your own size. You'll have tall, athletic, peace-loving, antiwar children together."

"And you, Rez?" James was suddenly all attention and the intense eyes bore down on Malek. "Did I see *you* in Baghdad? What were you doing there?"

"You already know what I was doing there."

"But I don't know much else about you, do I? You already know everything about my life. You met the old man and you came down to Virginia with me. You know I shot down my chances at this job here and that your own job is safe, and I'm happy for you and even happier for myself, because I wouldn't want to compete with you. And—"

"Is that why you did it? So you wouldn't take my job?"

"No. I did it because I lost something and thought I would find it here: purpose. But it's not here, it seems. So let's stop talking about me. Let's talk about you."

Malek had told him the outlines plenty of times already. Growing up in Tehran. The revolution. Life in Fresno, California, at the cookie shop with his dad. College. A fairly useless doctorate with a final PhD thesis on those God-crazy Sufis in Basra. Then back to the Middle East. The wars. Et cetera. He'd even told James about working with people like Clara Vikingstad in Tehran, Kabul, and Baghdad, but he hadn't mentioned the names of Sina and Fani, not even Soaad.

"There's nothing to say. Unlike you, I'm good here in Harlem. I like teaching, mostly. I can retire here, I don't mind."

"Fair enough. Let's retire then," James responded, getting up. "Let's go to your place and have us a few shots."

Malek followed. But then, as they came around to the main hall, there was a yell and they heard both of their names being called.

It was Candace Vincent. She was running toward them and Malek could already tell she must have been crying. It was late. Almost ten at night. The last classes of the evening had gotten out at nine fifteen and the halls in the ugly, prisonlike building with its labyrinth of dead corners and windowless rooms was deserted.

Candace Vincent came right up to the two men and stopped, staring at both of them with half-stunned eyes and breathing hard. Malek read the situation right away.

This was about her kids' pops, as she called him, the fellow who had gotten out of Rikers recently and was giving her trouble. She had written Malek about it again and wondered what she should do. He'd suggested that she go down to the college gym and look up his friend Professor McGreivy's new self-defense class. So she went, loved it, then wrote to Malek to tell him about the way Professor McGreivy would lead you through a move like you were born to do it, like anything was possible.

Now she stood there eyeing both men, panting, and then she broke into a welter of sobs.

It was James who reached out to her and drew her close. "Shh, you'll be all right now." He caressed her gently and said, "What did I tell you guys in class? There's nothing that can't be fixed, there's no hold that can't be broken."

Malek stood there and watched the two of them. He could already see where this moment would lead and maybe that was all right. Or maybe not. He wasn't even sure which one of their shoulders Candace had come to sob on. He was just glad that James had reached out first. Because that was what James McGreivy did. He did it for a living. He was no one if not that soldier directing traffic in Baghdad.

Clara Vikingstad was on TV again. She wore a tasteful black dress and had those gleaming eyes and that look of wise confidence which disarmed every interviewer who invited her on their show. She'd also had her black hair cut short since her brief arrest in Qum last summer. After coming back, she'd written a long piece about her fleeting experience in an Iranian jail, which was followed by appearances on the television talk circuit. Malek had called her one time in September but she hadn't gotten back to him yet.

She would. When it was time.

Malek muted the TV. Two weeks earlier Soaad had telephoned. Anna had died at the hospital on a night Soaad wasn't with her. They had taken her body away and buried it somewhere, but not at the Jewish cemetery. Now distant relatives of her late Iranian husband were showing up from nowhere and fighting over the possession of the apartment and the scant furniture in it.

On the phone Soaad had asked Malek if he'd managed to do anything with Anna's letter.

"What letter?"

"The one she gave you when you were here."

He'd come back to New York and left the letter Anna had dictated to Soaad on the empty bookshelf in the living room. Now he went over and took it out of the envelope and stood there examining it. He should not have forgotten Anna like that. She had just about begged to be buried in that Jewish cemetery they'd visited in Tehran. But according to Soaad, the hospital people had at first assumed they would be sending her body to the Christian cemetery. Then, realizing that her identity card showed she'd had to switch faiths to Islam to remain married to her husband, they'd dropped her at the sprawling Muslim cemetery in the south of the city.

And that was where Anna's body had finally gotten lost. The cemetery people had no record of where she was.

Anna, Malek thought, was the ultimate castaway. And he felt the full guilt of not having done something more for her when he could.

He said to Soaad, "Has that man bothered you?" He meant Fani, knowing Soaad understood exactly who he meant without having to spell it out on the phone.

"You mean bother me by coming around? No." There was a pause, and then Soaad added, "Yes, he has come around, but it wasn't a bother."

Malek felt a pang of fear, the kind you only feel for your own kin, your own flesh and blood. Which was still a new feeling for him. He asked her what she meant.

"He just came one day and said you hadn't returned his call."

It was true. On a Friday he had heard Fani's voice on his answering machine. All Fani said was, "Our mutual friend is nowhere to be found. This may cause some problems. Call!"

Malek hadn't called. He didn't want to give Fani the impression he was so invested in Sina's case.

And Sina really had disappeared. No contact from him since the end of the summer. Meanwhile, James McGreivy took up the space Sina had vacated. It was a peculiar shifting of characters in Malek's head. And he questioned, just slightly, its significance.

He heard Soaad whisper something on the phone and asked her to repeat it.

"Don't come back here," she said a bit louder. "You don't need to. I will be all right."

She had been forced to abandon him when he was a kid, and now she wanted to make a sacrifice of herself. He told her to stop it.

"I am sorry that your friend Anna died," he said. "I'll read her letter after we hang up."

"It's her life story."

"I know."

Ever since that phone call two weeks ago, books about World War II and the Holocaust had been slowly piling up in the middle of Malek's living room. Anna's letter, written in Soaad's careful Persian handwriting, told an abbreviated version of her journey, from a little town halfway between Bialystok and Warsaw, to Tehran in the years between 1939 and 1942. She'd been a kid, one of an impossibly huge exodus of Poles escaping first from Hitler and later from Stalin. In the end, from what Malek could tell in the books, about a hundred thousand of these refugees had shown up in Tehran. The Jewish kids among them would be carried off to what would soon become Israel, and they would be known from then on as the *Tehran Children*.

Malek tried to imagine a hundred thousand Poles in Iran in 1942. With Anna among them, hiding her Jewish identity and staying put in that faraway city all these decades. Anna, the last-known Jewish Pole of Tehran in 2008! She had dictated to Soaad, *Tehran was the first place after three years of hell where I felt some safety. I didn't want to leave it. I didn't know back then what awaited me anywhere else.* It was as if she was begging Malek to understand and excuse her for staying put, for not going to the Jewish homeland, for hiding who she was.

The story buried him and haunted him for days on end. He recalled the three of them in the Jewish cemetery that day. Had he really put his mind to it, he could have done something then. He could have arranged things so Anna would get buried there eventually. He knew people in Tehran and had plenty connections of his own. But somehow Anna's story just hadn't quite

stuck with him at the time. He had been too preoccu-
pied with Sina, and with Fani, to understand what it
meant for this woman to be buried in that place. And
now it was too late. He had failed her, and by failing her
he had failed Soaad.

On the muted TV, Clara and the interviewer had returned after a commercial break. Malek considered this
dance of improbabilities that surrounded him: Clara on
that television; Anna's story, which had made him go
on a spree of Holocaust books now scattered all over
the floor of his apartment; Sina under the radar somewhere in Iraq; and James McGreivy, the decorated Marine captain from Long Island and veteran of Fallujah,
now shacked up in a Bronx housing project with Candace Vincent and her kids.

Malek turned Clara off. He wasn't teaching tonight,
but decided to head for the college gym where he'd find
James. He figured he was obliged to have at least one
conversation with his friend about his new situation
with Candace before flying to Tehran in a few days.

Even as it began to happen, and before he actually took
a punch in the chest and fell on the stone steps of the
quad where a small bevy of students quickly ran to his
aid, Malek knew exactly what the situation was.

He was eventually helped up by two campus security
guards who eyed him like he had been hit just to make
their day especially difficult. The crowd was already
thinning and there was Candace standing ten feet away,
looking distraught but holding herself together: "Sorry,
professor. It's my fault. I'm the cause of all this."

Malek shook off the guards and went to sit on the

very steps he had just rolled off of. He'd been hit hard. His attacker was gone. Candace's former guy, the father to her kids.

His chest was in some pain. And there was a gash on the side of his head where he had first met pavement. As he rewound the past few minutes, he saw himself coming up to the Gothic structure where the college gym was housed. In front of it: Candace and a man she was arguing with. The man was about Malek's size. His head was closely shaved and he had a distinctive island accent. Not Jamaican. Maybe Trinidad. But it was Candace doing most of the arguing while the man seemed like he was actually trying to reason with her. She wanted him off her campus, Malek overheard. And then a smile coming across her face, saying, "Oh, hi, professor." Now the man turned and saw Malek standing there, frozen. The fellow had a chiseled jawbone. Big eyes. Handsome. And now he was coming up to Malek without a word, his right hand balling into a fist.

He wasn't even sure what he had come to tell James today. *Don't break my student's heart.* That was it. Because he wasn't sure if McGreivy planned to stay with her out of some momentary sense of duty or because he meant it.

And what business was it of Malek's, anyway?

He had been happy for them. That night when Candace came running down the hallway, James had ended up driving her home. And simply stayed. Soon he was Uncle James to Candace's boys. Helping them with their homework. Teaching them to wrestle and throw the football. He admitted to Malek that neighbors looked at him funny at first, but he'd grown on them. And there was no sign of the kids' father. Until today.

Candace was whispering something to him: "He's not a bad sort, he's just violent sometimes." Who was she talking about, the guy who had just hit him or James? The campus security people were telling him something too that he couldn't make out. He was thinking of being in Tehran so he could find Sina and be with Soaad and search for Anna's body. How was he going to find Anna's body in a city of fourteen million? And how stunning the two of them, Candace and James, appeared together on campus. They'd started showing up here holding hands, in defiance of all the vague, silly rules against professor-student relationships.

The fog in his head cleared. And suddenly Malek understood why, really, he had come to see James today: he wanted a happy ending. He wanted more than anything for this *thing* between the improbable couple to work out. Because if it did, it meant hope wasn't lost in this world. It meant Malek himself had a chance, and so did Soaad, and Sina, maybe even Anna.

He had, in essence, come to secure a guarantee from James McGreivy on behalf of his former student.

Malek and Candace both ended up having to give statements at the campus security office, where they asked Malek if he needed medical assistance or wanted the NYPD so he could charge the guy who had hit him. No, he said, and saw that Candace looked relieved. Let her kids' father think he'd taken his revenge. Let him also think he'd already broken parole with an assault. Then he just might put as much distance between himself and her as possible.

Back outside, he asked her, "You've been writing, Candace?"

"Always." She added, "Thank you for introducing James to me."

"What do you guys do together?"

"We talk. We take care of the kids. We live. I never had much of that. You hurt?"

"Maybe for a few days. Nothing that won't go away."

"I hope you find someone to love one day. I'll pray for you."

He nodded.

"My statement to the security," she reflected, "will it get James in trouble at school?"

"Even if it did, he can handle it. Your James, he's a tough man."

"He's the toughest man I ever met. And I've seen some real tough ones where I come from." She smiled.

A Spanish bar with the unlikely name of Katz sat a block away from the Jamaica Center subway. It was a few minutes' drive from JFK Airport and at night it filled up with Central American laborers.

It was also where Malek first stopped whenever he had to fly during the past couple of years. But this time James had insisted on driving him to the airport. Now a dozen empy shots of tequila and several beers sat between the two men. In front of them on a beat-up dance floor, a man with an outsize cowboy hat was desperately trying to get the waitress to dance with him while the jukebox played some aching south-of-the-border tune. And of all the things Malek could have recalled at that moment, he went back to those Kabul nights in the wealthy Wazir Akbar Khan District where you could drink yourself to an inch of your life at those wild parties under the auspices of one of the Coalition embassies, while not five blocks away Afghans died of everything you could possibly die of, including the freezing weather and hunger and disease and roadside bombs and guns and knives and heroin and lack of heroin and just plain good old-fashioned Afghan payback. It was a screwed-up, unjust world, and when a guy sat down in the Wazir Akbar Khan District to drink himself into a stupor, he either did it because, like a lot of those embassy paper-pushers, he couldn't care less, or because he simply didn't want to dwell anymore on what was happening five blocks away to his right and left. A man wanted to sit there while foreign whores served him Indian beer and Canadian whiskey so he could forget that Clara Vikingstad was up there in a warm room interviewing some UN apparatchik for the hundredth time about how awful war could get.

Malek thought, if this Mexican joint at the dog-end of Queens brought him back to that Kabul of a few years ago, only God would know what James McGreivy was thinking. Because the former soldier had to be thinking of something too. Maybe something as ordinary as: there was no way on earth he was going to drive anywhere after all the booze they'd had. And that was fine with Malek. James could sit here and piss till he was sober enough and Malek would just ride the train the rest of the way to the airport and get on that plane and fly to Tehran.

Then Malek simply blurted out over the music what had been on his mind all evening: "Have any of your own soldiers read your book?"

James turned to regard Malek. His eyes were bloodshot, but more from fatigue than alcohol; both of Candace's boys had come down with the flu and James had not had much sleep for the past few nights. McGreivy nodded his head. Yes, his soldiers had read the book, he seemed to say. And no, he didn't want to talk about it. He didn't want to talk about *that* because it was still too new. And because there were those under his command who had probably thought of him as some kind of prophet, and others who detested his particular brand of heroism. It was all in the book, anyway. He'd never questioned the bravery of his men, but he had rubbed salt in their wounds. Because . . . Fallujah had been no Iwo Jima; he had stuck to his guns about that. And for decades henceforth the men who had served with him would get heartburn every time James McGreivy's name came up—not because he might be telling the truth, but because he had infused the kernel of doubt in their Marine hearts, the poison of uncertainty that made each of them wonder if their valor had ever been worth anything.

During a pause after what seemed like the longest of Mexican love songs, James said, "I know Candace's ex was outside that gym wanting to have it out with me. I'm sorry you got punched instead, Rez."

Malek murmured that it was nothing.

"I guess I screwed it up, didn't I?" James smiled tiredly.

"The school contacted you?"

"Yeah. They want to know all kinds of things, like how come I'm running a self-defense class filled with women at the gym and why I'm going out with a student. Our favorite Texan has also called me to his office to have a little chat."

"You've done nothing wrong."

"They might not even let me finish the year."

"They will. They just won't renew your contract next year. You should have stuck to the military. Kill a few more *hajjis*, win a few more medals. You'd be a major now, sitting behind some desk, directing traffic from a distance, and giving PowerPoint lectures about urban warfare, proud of your accomplishments. Your old man would be happy too."

"That's not funny, Rez."

"Tell me, what are you doing with Candace Vincent?"

"Living the life I want."

"You're happy there in the Bronx?"

"It has to start somewhere, doesn't it? I mean, we can talk all we want about changing the world. But who's gonna do it?"

"Is that what you're doing, changing the world? That's what Candace Vincent and her kids are to you?"

"You know that isn't it."

"You love her?"

"I'm damaged goods, Rez. You've only known me a few months. But I'm doing well there in the Bronx for now. I like it. I know you don't believe me, but it's true."

"You love her?"

"I was ready to give something of myself in this life and she was ready to receive it."

"Like charity?"

"That's low, Rez."

"I'm just trying to understand."

James downed the last of his beer and banged the bottle with impatience. "Understand what? I couldn't tell you about love if it hit me in the face. But I do find myself in a situation that gives me satisfaction. It's good for me, it's good for her, it's good for the kids. Is there really something so wrong with that?" He leaned forward. "And I know what you're thinking. You're thinking, *Here's McGreivy. Just like America. Pushing his weight around, thinking he's bringing good to the world.* Isn't that it, Rez? But if it pleases you to hear it, then yes, I guess I am in love, in a way. I'm in love with a paradigm that works. Me and that girl, we work well together. I'm not even sure how in the hell it works so well. But it does. And that's all that matters to me. I can't go chasing after vague concepts. I'll take this thing I got right here and call it love if that pleases you. And I'll run with it."

"I'm glad to hear it then. That's all I wanted to know."

"Seriously?"

"It may come as a shock to you, but I really do care about the people I'm close to. I care about you. And I care about my former student. And if this thing is working, then the world isn't all shit."

"The world isn't all shit, Rez. There's just a lot of it to wade through sometimes till you're in the clear."

James stood up. He pointed to their empty bottles and then started toward the bar. They were sitting at a corner table and the waitress was too busy to pay them much attention. Malek only had a carry-on case and the flight was not for another four hours. By the time James returned to the table, he had already bought two Mexican men a round of drinks. You could see the marks of hard, honest labor on the men's faces. Malek watched James drink the round with them, slapping them on the back and shaking their hands. He talked to them in the language of men the world over, the brotherhood of tough work and play. James McGreivy knew something about these things. He was the champion of the underdog—the guy with less food, less clothes, less ammo. That was why the former Marine couldn't come to terms with Fallujah. He'd won the fight there in Iraq. But it hadn't been a fair fight. Not even close. And it was what he had to live with for the rest of his life. So perhaps he would marry Candace Vincent and move her and the kids back to Long Island, while the men he had gone to officer training with went on to polish their medals and write expert monographs on fighting terror.

The night turned liquid in Malek's head. He was grateful that James McGreivy existed in this world. And suddenly he was terribly afraid of losing this American whom he hadn't even known half a year. The feeling made him sentimental. And when James asked him again to tell the truth about why he was going to Tehran, Malek just admitted it. He began with Soaad. And before long he had told James about Fani, who held the key to the release of Soaad's dossier, and finally, slowly, like a man who feels himself inexorably tiptoeing into the abyss, he told James about Sina Vafa, his best friend from college.

Malek didn't even bother to raise his head when James quietly got up and went for a final round. He plopped two more shots on their table. "Last call, friend!"

Out on the floor, with the bopping blue and red lights chasing the whirl and spin of the dancers, the waitress had finally given in to the pleading of one of the men and began to dance with him.

Malek said, "You must understand, Sina Vafa is try-ing to save the world just like you. The two of you are not that different from each other."

It was only half a joke. But even as he'd started to say it, Malek came to believe it. He waited, with more con-viction than he had energy for, to see what James would say about that.

"I don't know what your friend is doing in Iraq. What I know is men like him were the cause of the death of my men."

"I doubt it."

"If you're sitting here tonight to defend that son of a bitch, then why even tell me about it?"

Malek thought about it. He had no answer. And his mood was turning again. James McGreivy was no longer the man he would have taken a bullet for only a half hour ago. He was, actually, something of an enemy. Maybe. Malek wasn't sure about anything. His head was foggy. He had to take that plane to Tehran in three hours.

"I said he's involved in something. I don't know what."

"The bullets coming my way over there didn't have *Shia* or *Sunni* written on them. They killed either way. You *wanted* me to know this. You've been damn near ex-ploding to tell someone about it. And now you have."

"What do you want me to do about it?"

"Talk to the man. Tell him to cease and desist. Tell him it's not his fight."

"How do you know it's not his fight? Maybe it is."

That was the crux of it. Maybe it actually was Sina's fight. And James McGreivy and Reza Malek, who had both written about that fight, sat staring at each other in the Spanish bar until neither of them could stand it anymore.

Malek finally asked, "What will you do about it?"

"Me? It's not my fight anymore."

SOAAD

They were in a cemetery again. Outside on the coast road, a flood of flag-waving cars rushed in a cacaphony to the Anzali stadium for the weekend soccer match. Inside the Christian cemetery, though, things were serene. An Armenian family stood above a plot and would glance benignly over at Malek and Soaad, who strolled through the large section devoted to the Poles of World War II. There were about eight hundred Polish tombstones here, and unlike the Jewish cemetery in Tehran, all of them seemed to bear Christian names.

It had been on Soaad's insistence that they come. She said she wanted to see everything that had to do with Anna. Which was hardly possible. But coming here was something they could do. So Malek had hired a car and a driver from Tehran, and they'd spent the night in a hotel before coming to the cemetery in the morning. Soaad had bought flowers. And now she dropped to her knees and lovingly lay the stems of very expensive white orchids on an arbitrary grave. It happened to be the grave of a Polish child who had died in 1942.

Malek noticed once again how lithe and supple his mother was. He'd thought that Anna's death might break her. Now he saw that this woman, at sixty, was pretty much unbreakable. For four days straight she had made him come with her to the Behesht Zahra Cemetery of Tehran to see if they could find Anna, whose corpse was still lost in that immense place. Soaad wasn't pushy, but was relentless in the way only someone who has known prison can be. On the fourth day, the petty cemetery official told them to go away and not come back; they had no idea where this Anna woman was, and since no close relatives had shown up with documents, there would not be an investigation to find her.

"Somebody will steal those orchids," Malek said.

Soaad got up and turned to her son. He saw the contentment in her face. She had been waiting for him to return so she could buy orchids, Anna's favorite flower, and put them on some grave, any grave, but preferably one that had something to do with Poland.

"You know," she said, "Anna always mentioned Poland like she preferred not to talk about it."

Malek pointed toward the Caspian shore, a stone's throw from where they stood. "This port is where the Poles came when they arrived from Russia. Right where we're standing. A lot of them had typhus by the time they got here. That's why there are so many graves."

"They suffered, didn't they?"

A new wave of cars rushed past the cemetery heading for the stadium. Interestingly, the local team was playing against Sina's family's old team. You could have gotten yourself killed if you wore the red colors of Sina's team in Anzali today. And yet the team's supporters were bound to show up. There would be fights. For a moment Malek had the absurd notion that maybe Sina would be among them.

"I mean," she went on, "I know they suffered. It was

all Anna wanted to talk about during her last weeks. But I didn't know there were so many like her."

He condensed the story of those years and all those refugees into five minutes in that graveyard. The gist of it was that Anna's family were among the Jews who had ended up in the Russian gulags instead of the German concentration camps. That was what had saved Anna: the gulag! Then another year of starvation in Central Asia after they'd been released. The rest of it Soaad already knew because she had written down what Anna had dictated to her. How in Tashkent Anna's family had taken her to a Christian orphanage run by freed Poles. As a Christian, Anna had been put on a ship and brought to Iran. In the Tehran camps, she had been too embarrassed to suddenly admit she was a Jew. The other Jewish kids had been taken away to Palestine. She'd stayed. Turned into a Christian. Then a Muslim.

Her story was like a lost boat. And even now her dead body was lost in Tehran somewhere. Those kids who made it to Israel may have been called the Tehran Children, but Anna was the ultimate Tehran child. And she would never leave it.

Soaad insisted that they walk along the beach by the Anzali port, just to see exactly where Anna might have disembarked.

On the beach he let her move ahead and made a long-distance call on his cell phone to America. Surprisingly, a little boy's voice answered James's phone. One of Candace's, Malek assumed. This brought a smile to his face and he hung up.

When he caught up to Soaad, she held his hand and said, "We have been watched ever since you arrived."

"Yes, we have." He was stunned. He had not expected her to notice. Not even when the same motorcycle rider followed them two days in a row to the cemetery in Tehran. He had considered it might be Sina. But it wasn't.

She said, "It's me, isn't it? I'm the one causing you this headache."

"I'm going to take you to America with me."

"At what price?"

"Whatever price has to be paid is not mine to pay. You are simply a guarantee in lieu of something else."

"Why are they following us then?"

"They want to see if I know where Sina is. Once they are sure I don't know, they'll come forward."

"What has your friend gotten himself into?"

Malek sighed. "We all get ourselves into something sooner or later. You got yourself into something way back then and it's still with you. Anna, she told a lie one day in some orphanage in Russia, and except for you and me, she had to take it to the grave with her." He kept himself from adding, *And we don't even know where that grave is.* "As for Sina, he's into something now. And so it goes."

"What are you into then?"

He considered that. "I'm not sure yet. But I'll know soon enough."

Soaad then uttered that she loved him, her only son. And he held her to his chest and said he knew this, and that in the end it would be all right.

They had agreed to meet at the teahouse across from Sina's building. It was early afternoon and the place was crowded. A couple of young laborers lay sleeping on benches near the window, weak winter sun shining on their faces. They reminded Malek of those two Mexican men James had bought drinks for at that bar in New York.

Fani came through the door.

"Are you being followed these days?" Malek asked right away.

"Ever since your friend Sina's case has acquired the attention of the powers that be, I am no longer followed. I'm just another man on payroll."

"So you will not make the fortune you thought you would from Sina's portfolio?"

"I will," Fani said easily, "but I will have to share. That's how it is here." He didn't seem in the mood for the usual chitchat. He appeared focused and ready to get on with business.

"Who is following *me* then?"

"My people."

"Look, I don't know where Sina is."

"I know. Which makes it all the more important you devote the next week to me. We need some more signatures from you."

Malek looked squarely in Fani's eyes. "I have a request in return."

"Make your request."

"I spoke to Sina's mother. She and her husband have found a piece of Vafa property. They too need a signature from me. It's only a single piece of property. It's not much, by your standards."

"I already know about it. You may sign off on that property. I don't need it."

"You mean you won't try to take it from them?"

"If I wanted to, I would have done so by now. Think of it as my gift to you."

"So will I still be followed?"

Fani got up. "You'll know whenever you are." He gave an address for Malek to be at early the next day. It was one of those quasi law offices where deeds and properties changed hands in three-foot-long handwritten ledgers.

Malek doubled and tripled back on himself for two hours until he was absolutely sure no one was following him. Back in New York, knowing what was probably in store for him, he had bought a dubious book with a chapter about evasion tactics. The book was mostly silly, spy-movie mumbo jumbo, but there were also nuggets of useful information that, put together, came in handy.

He now emerged from the depths of the brass-sellers quarter of the sprawling Grand Bazaar wearing a cap and a cheap navy-blue windbreaker he had just bought and hailed a motorcyclist who took him halfway to his destination. From there he hopped in a regular cab and went all the way to a part of the city most people never saw. It was close to the Rey District near a park that only junkies frequented, the kind of place cops would raid once a month to fulfill their quotas. Most of the addicts were harmless men with more philosophy in them than danger. One time, when a French documentary filmmaker had needed a translator, Malek had spent a good two weeks in the area. It was a world unto itself. The railroad tracks going south were just on the other side of the highway, with a shantytown traveling the length of the tracks. Here, laborers, drug dealers, prostitutes, and men off the bus from their villages for the very first time lived crowded lives that went nowhere quickly. Children played with their homemade kites on the tracks and chickens clucked back and forth as trains lumbered by.

The woman who the whole park called *Maman* was sitting where she always sat, on a bench where she could have a fair view of all the angles when the police decided to pay her a visit.

Her trained eyes quickly realized it was Malek walking up to her, and she broke into a toothless smile. She never forgot a face or a name. She never sold bad dope. She never informed on anyone.

"Aqa Malek! And in a hurry. Why?"

Malek kissed her hand and handed Maman her weakness, a bar of Toblerone chocolate—one of those large ones you could only get in airports.

"I'm looking for the Afghan."

She peered into the distance, her mind an inexhaustible thread of what-ifs and broken promises and a long-dead junkie husband who had first turned her on to the habit. On rainy nights the other addicts who had nowhere to sleep would crowd her and she would quote off the top of her head classical Persian poems from Hafiz and Rumi into the wee hours of the morning.

"The Afghan prospers." She gave Malek an address. "You'll be stopped down there. Give them my name." She hesitated a moment and then added, "How is America?"

"It's a bit like a habit."

"Do you like your habit?"

"It's not out to kill me."

"Go with God then."

* * *

The address Maman had given him was a twenty-minute walk. Malek stepped into a narrow alley and lounging men gave him the once-over. There were maybe a half-dozen areas in Tehran like this that he knew of, places that were usually no-go for the police. Boys no older than nine stood inside shacks pimping their twelve-year-old sisters. Men in debt came out of two-table teahouses with puffy opium faces. And above it all, instead of flashing neon, tall black standards with the names of the Shia martyrs draped the sides of hole-ridden walls.

It took a kid scout and then another before Malek was brought to a man who introduced himself as Khiyaal. The man resembled an industrial-sized fridge and his name, which meant *Imagine*, left a lot to wonder about. There was another hour of waiting. The sky grew dark and a winter chill sat inside Malek's bones. They were in the back of a kebab house where Afghan men sat in huddles chatting quietly and drinking tea. The dank place smelled of sweat and war and furtiveness. It was everything that Malek had wanted to never return to. Yet here he was. Again. His phone rang and he retreated to a corner to answer it, guessing from the strange numbers who it was.

James spoke without a hello. "My kid answered the phone the other day. Sorry! I knew it was you. I wasn't sure the number you'd given me would work, but hey, here you are."

Malek considered what James had said. *My kid*. The words sounded so natural over that phone. So right. The man could make a believer out of anyone. Still, Malek flipped the little foldout phone shut. Speaking English would bring undue attention at this fence-shop in the rat's end of the city of Tehran. He hadn't wanted to do this, look up any old associates. But there was no helping it. If anyone could help him locate Sina, it would be the man everybody else simply knew as the Afghan, but whom Malek and Sina had once known as Babur.

To look at Babur you would have thought he could be knocked over with the fat pinky finger of his current lieutenant, Khiyaal. But Babur, who barely reached to Malek's chest and was as thin as the thinnest junkies in Maman's park, was one of those free agents who are natural at staking territory wherever they go. It was in the Badakhshan Province in Afghanistan the first time that Malek and Sina had come upon the Afghan. He was running then, from the Taliban fundamentalists fighting the Americans, *and* from the Americans. Years earlier, before the Americans' arrival, Babur had secured himself the unlikeliest job in the world: a cook at one of the camps in southern Afghanistan where the Arab, Chechen, and Bosnian fighters came to get training for their various holy wars. The Arabs bosses of the camps strictly forbade communication between the foreign fighters and the local Afghans. So Babur had played deaf and dumb. Literally. Which made him an ideal servant in the eyes of the men who ran the camp. Until one time somebody had caught him late at night in bed listening to a faint radio station coming out of India. The next day they would surely cut his throat for lying to them. So Babur had hit the road. To Pakistan, then India. In Bombay he'd done every kind of job for Muslim mobsters until somebody from back in Afghanistan recognized him. Then he was on the run again. Back to the old country and to the Badakhshan Province, where he took a chance and told his tale to Malek and Sina who befriended him. They'd smuggled him with them back to Iran, the one place neither the Americans nor the Taliban could follow him. And here, in the last few years, was where he'd built himself a fat business working the cheap Afghan labor market and dealing in stolen goods. He was a little Afghan lord now. And he owed Malek a lot. Malek had never called in a chip. And maybe he wasn't calling in one now. All he wanted to know was where he could find Sina Vafa.

"I hear strange things about him," Babur was saying.

Babur had come in, embraced Malek, and signaled to follow him to the second floor of the kebab house. The man who brought them plates of rice and yogurt had an angelic face but no ears. A throwback to the time of the Soviet war in the '80s when some of the more fanatical muj commanders would cut off the ears of any child they found going to the godless schools of the infidels.

"What do you hear?" Malek asked.

Babur fidgeted in his seat. He had hardly changed. Still thin as a wraith, with flashing wide, intelligent eyes that saw everything before others. In Badakhshan he had taken one glance at Malek and Sina in that little end-of-the-earth marketplace and knew he could trust them with his story. Now it was Malek who needed to trust someone.

"Aqa Malek, I have love for you. And I have a good life now in Tehran."

"Then don't tell me anything that might cause you trouble."

Babur went to scoop some rice with his hand, then changed his mind and looked up at Malek. "You? You are in trouble?"

"No. But tell me about Sina."

"Tell me about yourself first."

Malek sighed. "I have a mother."

"Mothers are good, my brother."

"I may need to smuggle her out of the country."

"Consider it done."

"She has a file."

Babur froze for just a moment. "With who?"

"With people who can make life very difficult for you if they learn you smuggled her out."

"You are my brother. I will still do it for you when and if you ask."

Malek breathed deeply, not sure if it was relief he was feeling or a new level of apprehension. "I am also looking for a dead body."

Babur almost swallowed the little Persian cigarette he'd been trying to light instead of eating his rice. "You have lost your mind, like our good friend Sina."

"Nothing like that. It has to do with my mother again. Her friend died. Some Polish lady called Anna. They lost her body at the big cemetery, if you can believe it. The fools! I want to make my mother happy and find the body. I need a grave for Anna."

"You love your mother that much, Aqa Malek."

Malek shrugged. For some reason he was thinking about Sina's mother, and what Sina and Fani had done to her and her husband years ago, kicking them out of their house.

"All right. We will make a grave for Anna," Babur announced.

"But the body?"

Babur's expression said it all. "Aqa Malek, do you

know how many bodies never make it to the grave in this world?" He pointed to the earless guy who was working quietly in the back kitchen. "For every one of those men walking around Afghanistan today, a hundred of them had their ears cut off only after they were killed and chopped up. No one knows where they are. No one cares. Do you think Anna cares? Anna doesn't care. What is this Anna's last name?"

"She was married to an Iranian once. Last name was Majidi."

"Beautiful. Mrs. Anna Majidi. We will fix it. It will cost some money. Grave plots are not cheap these days."

Malek took out a wad of hundred-dollar bills and gave fifteen of them to Babur. "Fix it as best you can."

Babur took the money and stuffed it in his pocket. "Now, who else do you love, Aqa Malek?"

"I love Sina Vafa."

"The man has a price on his head in south Afghanistan, especially around Kandahar. Did you know that?"

"I did not know."

"Don't forget I was a cook for these people way back then. The camps of those days, they will never be repeated. No one will ever get that kind of training again." Babur shook his head, almost nostalgic. "Those men, they may have been many things. But men they were. And they hated Iranians." He laughed. "Called you people *innovators*. Worse than Jews. Worse than Christians. Your friend Sina had it in his head to make contact with people like that. He was going around Kandahar, where everybody and their mother is a spy, advertising that a Muslim is a Muslim, Shia and Sunni do not matter. It's a miracle he didn't get killed there and then."

"Who wants him dead over there?"

"Whoever. Maybe Sunnis. Maybe some man sitting in an office in London who is worried about the safety of his contractors in Kandahar. I can give you a list of a hundred men off the top of my head who have prices on their heads in Afghanistan. Sina is just one of them. And it's not even a high price."

"Where do I find him?"

"If he's not dead."

"Babur, you of all people would know if he's dead."

"He has been playing with men whose shadows scare me. I'm just a poor Afghan trying to survive in Tehran."

Malek stood up, exhausted but also satisfied. Babur knew exactly where Sina was. Malek had come to the right person. Sina may have even counted on Malek coming here. The Afghan was the one trustworthy connection to the underworld that they both shared. Babur knew all right. And all this talk today had conveyed to Malek that he knew without actually spelling it out for him.

Malek walked to the stairway.

Babur didn't get up. "Aqa Malek!" he called. Malek turned. "Don't come back here!"

"You'll find me?"

"Yes, I'll find you when the time is right."

"Just remember, I'm not here long, Babur."

"We'll start with the grave for Mrs. Anna. What was her last name again?"

Saidi!

Malek cursed the Afghan for having remembered Anna's husband's last name wrong. Now he and Soaad stood in a corner of the vast cemetery, surrounded by a sea of dead with a misspelled gravestone and Soaad laying orchids on it anyway. Malek let his mother have her time, acting like she didn't really care about the mistake.

It was a poorly kept area. Wind seemed to carry grocery bags from miles away and drop them at exactly this spot, so that the graves seemed like they had plastic blooming out of them.

Anna Saidi.

The wrong name, the fake burial, and the dance and twirl of ten thousand grocery bags in this part of the cemetery made everything about the woman's history seem like a terrible joke. And yet Malek remained quite still as his mother went about patiently clearing all the plastic from the immediate vicinity of Anna's plot.

Meantime, Babur still had no location on Sina.

Soaad said, "When they killed him, I didn't have a body that time either."

It took a few seconds for Malek to register what she meant. When they'd executed her second husband during the revolution, they'd probably dumped the body in some mass grave with others like him.

All Malek could say was, "I'm sorry. I tried." He was curious though. "But why do you lay the flowers if you know this is not her grave?"

"Because it gives me satisfaction. Thank you for this."

Twilight. It came early this season. And today it was a particularly stunning drift of filleted, salmon-colored clouds that seemed to stretch from here all the way to Arabia. Malek gazed at that sky. Winter cold sealing and tinting the noxious air of the city under a sphere of terrible beauty. It was poetry. All of it. This isolated cemetery plot of plastic garbage bags and leaning graves and a false tombstone. He glanced at his mother and he understood. Satisfaction was in the heart. He would not forget this moment at this hour in this spot. He would hold onto it like a meditation and relive it now and then, forever, like a prayer.

He left her at the apartment and took a cab to Sina's place. He hadn't been there yet on this trip, but still had the key. Surprisingly, the key worked. Though the place itself was entirely empty. Everything was gone. The exercise weights, the books, the guitar, bed . . . everything. He stood at the balcony watching the wrestlers and weight lifters down below for a while. Then, when he came out of the building, Fani was, as usual, waiting for him.

"Find something?" Fani asked.

"It's empty."

They drove. The evening traffic was heavy. Three days earlier Malek had signed a document that would allow Fani to work on the release of real estate in north Tehran belonging to Sina's father that was worth tens of millions of dollars. It was a sweet deal because in Tehran property, more than anything else, mattered. The confiscated Vafa estates in the land-hungry city were such an orgy of money and potential money that after a while you started to dream about it. You woke up thinking real estate and cash and who to bribe and how much of a cut to take for yourself.

Fani said, "You and your mother have a thing for cemeteries."

After a resigned pause, Malek answered, "It calms us down."

"I want you back in Tehran in the early summer. That is when our labors will bear fruit. By then those lands will be released, and you will come to sign for their sale."

"I don't trust you."

"I can live with that."

"You backed out of our deal about Sina's mother. You said you'd let her have that small piece of land that she and her husband found. Yesterday I went to court with them. The judge changed his mind. You did this. That old couple, I couldn't look them in the face. I almost had to carry them out of that courthouse."

"Yes, I did change the judge's mind. Temporarily."

"But why? What have that man and woman done to you?"

"Nothing. I feel for them. I had a mother myself once. Like you have a mother. Like Sina has a mother."

"What are you saying?"

"Only this: that I was Sina's case officer once. Let's not forget. I know his psychology. He is a man full of remorse. For his mother. For what he did to her before. If I let her have that property now, Sina will feel his conscience eased and he will be ready to die. He will get on with this martyrdom business that, to be honest, I find boring. So I put a stop to the transaction. For now. When our business, yours and mine, is done, that lady and her husband may have that piece of property."

"Sina doesn't want to die. He only wants to kill. Suicide is not his issue at all."

"This I understand. But sometimes a man who is so

focused on killing can end up killing himself. I cannot permit such stupidity at this time. Malek *jaan*, at the end of the day, our religion is simply a set of laws. And I am simply not able to work on the property of a dead man. The courts will not allow it, no matter who I know or who I have behind me. Then the Vafa estate will tumble into another cycle of negotiations and recriminations between men far above my station. I have no time for that. I am ready now. Not fifteen years from now."

Everything Fani said had truth to it. But Malek gave it another shot: "You are assuming Sina is still alive even as we speak."

Fani looked at Malek, reached over, and opened the passenger door. "Go to your mother, Mr. Malek. Make up for the lost years."

"You are acting like a thug, Fani!"

"I believe Sina Vafa is still alive. Should you find him before me, let him know that it will not do to get himself killed. He may do it a year from now when our business is done. But not this year. This year he must live and breathe. And I need you here in Tehran when I send the word. This is how the world turns. I will see you here in the summer. And stop going to so many cemeteries and spending so much money on orchids. It makes me depressed."

"At least let me take my mother out of the country."

"Your mother will go with you when our business is finished."

When Malek got out of the car, he saw Soaad standing in front of her building, holding a long piece of fresh *barbari* bread, watching them. Malek stuck his head back into the car. "Do I have your word?"

"About what exactly?"

"About letting my mother go when we are finished. Do I have your word on that?"

"This is Tehran, Malek *jaan*. Here, the last person you should ever trust is a man who looks you in the eye and gives you his word."

Soaad said, "I am selling this apartment. I have a buyer."

They sat in the kitchen. It was early morning, not quite light out. Malek had an eye on the small satellite TV that sat in a corner of the cabinet. A Persian news channel was repeating the programming from the previous afternoon; Clara was being interviewed on some Iranian TV station in California. She looked bright-eyed and had that slightly benevolent appearance she always assumed when being interviewed by non-American television stations.

Malek sipped his tea. "Who are you selling the apartment to?"

"Your friend, the Afghan."

He didn't bother asking her how she had come to know the Afghan. Soaad had turned out to be something of a pro. Even when she was being conned into giving meaningless reports to the intelligence people thirtysome years ago, she had remained cool about it. This thought made him love her more. Made him love her in a way he had never loved another woman.

He asked, "Do you think you've been followed lately?"

"I always know when I'm followed. It's a habit that never went away. We haven't been followed since we went to pay our respects to Anna."

"That wasn't Anna."

"It was Anna enough."

"What about the Afghan?"

"He made me memorize an address." She recited it. "Do you recognize it?"

"No. But I know whose it must be."

"I like your Afghan friend. He said that you saved his life once. He said he would do anything for you. I believe him. He said that I should be ready because he might be taking me out of the country. I told him I would have to sell my house, but discreetly. He said he would have someone buy it from me. But only for half what it is worth."

"Great friend I have."

"Men do what they can, Reza *jaan*. By summer, when you return, my house will be sold. I will be ready to go." She added, "If you still want me."

Malek gazed at her. "You never use more words than are necessary. How come?"

It was true. There was some kind of maximum efficiency about Soaad's way of talking. Its sparseness negated the maddening baroqueness of the Persian language. She had reduced her world to as little as possible—to him, to her yoga practice, to remembering her friend Anna.

"Words kill," she said. "I should know."

He was back in the Rey District. It was another *halabiabad*, a shantytown of improvised buildings mostly made of stolen brick and discarded metal. In a makeshift shack with salvaged chairs and desks, Sina Vafa was holding a class of sorts. There was a small blackboard resting against a precarious wall. Sina wrote out the letters of the Latin alphabet and made the six boys pronounce them loudly. It was curious how intently the kids were studying those letters. Sina's beard had grown a good two inches. His eyes were subdued, content. Malek had never seen him like this. The man he had known half a year ago was suddenly transformed. One door away, closer to the railroad tracks, a one-eyed teenage boy ran a small stand for Sina where they sold cigarettes, juice, ice cream, and a few other basic goods. On the other side of the schoolhouse Malek had gotten a glimpse of Sina's own room, not much bigger than a jail cell, with just some blankets and pillows neatly folded to the side. No sign of Sina's guitar or his books.

A half hour later the lesson was finished and four of the kids ran out by themselves. A couple of them waited for their parents to come get them. One of the parents, a war vet with a missing leg, arrived last bearing a fold of bread wrapped in a white cloth under one arm. He smiled at Sina, addressed him as Doctor Jalali, and gave him the bread, inviting him to drop by their "humble abode" tomorrow.

"So you've retired from Iraq, *Doctor Jalali*?" was the first thing Malek asked when they were alone.

"All this is very new." Sina made a wide gesture at the classroom and outside. "Even Babur doesn't believe me. Says I'm just playing make-believe and that I'll go back to my bad old ways soon enough."

"Are you playing make-believe?"

"No." The moment got washed in the noise of a passing train screeching a long whistle. Sina motioned for Malek to follow him out.

They stood there as the train slowly rumbled south.

When it was gone they could see the one-legged father and his boy receding on the other side of the tracks, the father working his crutch like a champ, every once in a while bending down to say something to his kid who would then run in circles around him and throw shadow punches.

This was the very end of Tehran—a place of love, like that father and child, and of relaxed misfortunes.

Malek's eyes fell on a junkie leaning against a lamppost. Kids with sticks would gather around, poke him, and run off.

"I've never been happier," Sina said. "If they just let me keep what I have here, I lack for nothing else."

"Who is *they*?" Malek asked when they were in the back area of the shack where Sina slept.

There was a knock on the door. A large woman, accompanied by a young girl, tumbled inside, loudly calling Sina "Mr. Doctor." Malek stood to the side, nonplussed. She was complaining of bad vision and dizzy spells. Sina went at it right away. He got a bag from under the sink, opened it, and began shining a light into the old woman's eyes and asking questions. Five minutes later, when the examination was done, woman and girl stood up and pretended to be about to drop some paper money into an empty glass jar near the door. Sina wouldn't let them, so they thanked the doctor again and walked out.

"She shows up every few days," Sina explained. "She needs glasses. I've told her so. But she likes to come anyway and have me shine that light in her eyes. It's our little ritual."

"*Doctor?*"

"She also has an older daughter. Husband disappeared six years ago. She's as beautiful as the moon, Rez. Our visitor wants me to ask for her daughter's hand. And you know what? I just might."

"Tell me about being a doctor."

"I had to learn basic field medicine. Goes a long way around here."

Malek gave the place another once-over. It really did seem like a jail cell. "I don't suppose you have a drink here?"

"For you, I have better. Sit!"

He hadn't smoked opium in a long time. The smoke was instantaneous in its effect. Every cell in Malek's body absorbed it and six months of anxiety seemed to lift and disappear after the first hit. Opium could be a friend that way. The room grew and Malek just lay there on the carpeted floor with one hand under his chin, listening to trains coming and going, children screaming, mothers calling their kids, life happening.

Sina served him from a charcoal burner. And it was as if Malek had really come on this trip to just lie here and smoke. He wanted to never leave and could understand perfectly why Sina had "retired." Malek could see himself living here. Teach English for free and maybe dispense a few aspirins now and then. Get himself a local woman whose husband had disappeared or overdosed. He had found Sina again, Sina who had first taken him to Kabul and to Baghdad. Sina who had sat bored stiff in those literature courses they took in college, complaining about the foolishness of going to school. Sina who had wanted to do something real with his life. Sina who had hated America, the very America that had taken him in and saved him. Sina who could sing country-and-western ballads with an unbelievable twang, but who now, with his sun-worn face and beard and loose-fitting white shirt, resembled the guy who might lead the Friday prayer at the local mosque.

Malek got more sappy with each hit of the opium. He had love for Sina, and for Soaad and Captain James McGreivy. Loving was good.

At some point his host left him alone to get some *aab-goosht* for them to eat. When he returned, Malek had been drifting in and out of sleep, the state of nodding that was nothing but sweet and made the world utterly tolerable. Sina laid the food next to the charcoal and urged him to dig in.

Malek was lying flat on his back engrossed in a paint bubble on the ceiling. He didn't move. "I imagine it must get hot here during the summer."

"Say what's on your mind," Sina prodded.

"I told someone about you. And not just anyone."

"Good."

Sina hadn't missed a beat with his response. Soon they were both lying flat on their backs and probably staring at the same paint bubble.

"Good?" Being on opium time, it took Malek what seemed like hours, but was really only minutes, to figure out the maze that had brought them here. "You whore's son," he said lovingly, switching to Persian for a moment, "you actually set me up to snitch on you. Why would you do that?"

"I have to kill myself off, Rez. I mean, I need to die on paper, the Iraqi rumor mill has to believe I'm really and truly dead. It would help me if the news comes from an American source. In fact, it can only come from an

American source." There was a long pause before Sina added, "Look, you wrote a book about the war. I figured you know people in the business over there."

"I don't know anyone."

"How about Clara Vikingstad?"

Malek smiled. Clara wouldn't have been the best medium for this kind of deception and Sina knew it. You could use journalists for all kinds of disinformation, but there was always a price to pay. The biggest price was this: with Clara's crowd, things often just got too loud.

Had it simply been coincidence that he had told James and not Clara about Sina? Or could Sina and his people play this deep a hand? The thought didn't quite unsettle Malek. He felt too good to be unsettled right now. But he did wonder if they had known all along there would be a new guy called Captain James Mc-Greivy teaching in Malek's department.

"I told a colleague of mine at college. A former Marine captain. A decorated guy."

"Why did you tell him about me?"

"I got drunk my last night before I got on the plane. What you'd been doing weighed heavy on me, Sina. I had to tell someone. So I told the one person I thought might have an inkling of what I was talking about."

"You did good."

Good? This, Malek thought, must be one of those beautiful moments. Two people who for two decades had been as close as blood suddenly realizing they have betrayed each other. And yet there is still love.

"If you wanted out of this business," Malek asked, "why not just stay away from it? Will QAF not let you?"

"They'll let me. As long as I keep quiet here in my little hovel. They always know where to find me."

"Fani knows where you are too?"

"If he tries hard enough he'll know. Nothing and no one stays hidden here too long."

"Then why give me power of attorney at all? Why not do what you have to do yourself?"

"Two reasons. One, I discovered your mother existed. And I wanted you to know about her."

"So it was just a favor to me?" Malek laughed lightly, his eyes half open. He felt like eating but couldn't muster the effort to sit up.

"Two, I don't know how long I'll be alive."

"Because of that dumb contract on your life in Kandahar? The Afghan told me about it. I wouldn't worry about that. Even Babur says there are bigger fish than you who need to be hunted. Don't take yourself so seriously."

"It's not death I'm afraid of. I got myself in trouble in Iraq, not Kandahar. An Arab girl. Beautiful. Sunni. Up there in Kirkuk. You know how the rest goes."

"Is she still alive?"

"No. Her brother had her killed because of me."

"You say it as if it means nothing to you."

"It means everything to me," Sina said, his voice breaking slightly.

Malek watched him jump to his feet to light a cigarette. The room wasn't warm and when Sina opened the door cold air rushed inside. It was dark out, except for the two crooked streetlamps that gave off weak light. You could still hear the sound of children playing soccer somewhere beyond the shadows. Farther away there was also the wail of more than one police car.

Light-headed, Malek forced himself up and joined Sina at the door. "I'm sorry."

"I had to work with all kinds of unpleasantness in Iraq. I mean, some real brutes. Then, in the middle of all this ugliness, something happened. Don't ask me how. Her brother—we'd been working with him and his people, though they hated Iranians way more than they hated Americans. They found out about us, me and her. I'm a fool for thinking they wouldn't. The rest . . . I don't know." Sina gave a light kick to the door and the two men stood listening to the distant whistle of a train moving farther away.

"This is why you need to be dead? They're still after you? It's a matter of honor for them?"

"The hell with their honor."

"That's why you went to Kurdistan in the summer. You wanted to try to take the brother out and finish this business."

Sina turned to him. "What was I supposed to do? I wanted to try everything before pulling you into my mess. Except my people didn't like that. They ordered me to go home and disappear for a while. So here I am, a sitting duck, and you have my power of attorney."

"Come on! It's not so hard for your people to spread a rumor in Iraq that you got killed."

"No one will believe it. Only if the Americans kill somebody they think is me will the rumor hold. People don't doubt the Americans that way. They know if the Americans count a kill, it's probably true."

Malek could tell Sina was waiting for some kind of answer. They couldn't just walk away from this and leave the decision for another day.

Sina continued, "I don't have to tell you what it's like over there. We had to work with everyone—Shia, Sunni, Kurd, doesn't matter. It's blood for blood with all of them. The bastard kills his own sister and is convinced it's my fault. So now it's my turn or they won't rest. And they won't work with us. Rez, if you help me . . ."

"I'll be saving your life."

"I don't want to die."

Malek felt his head spinning again and he had to squat down. "Do you know what you're asking me to do?"

"I'm asking you to make sure your captain friend tells somebody about me. One of his former colleagues, for example." Sina rested his hand on Malek's shoulder. "Explain to him that I'm one of the people targeting their private contractors in Iraq. You think you can do this for me?"

It was an operation. It had been thought through. It wasn't some off-the-cuff thing that they had devised to get this honor-bound Sunni guy and his clan in Iraq to lay off of Sina Vafa. It was important for someone that Sina not die. Not yet, anyway. Maybe that was why Fani had shown all those videos of private American security men in Iraq, saying they were from Sina's computer. Malek's high was lifting, as was his love. He felt sickness come over him—not necessarily for Sina and the needless web of lies he had laced around himself. It was more of a general revulsion; it was for this Middle East that always disappointed you, always made you grow extra eyes and stay suspicious.

"You want me to use James. That's what you want."

"That's his name? James?"

"He's my friend." Malek took Sina's hand off his shoulder.

"I'm your friend."

"And you're planning to set up some guy to take the fall for you in Iraq. The Americans will kill someone thinking they killed you. What if they don't kill him? What if they just arrest the guy and find out he's not you? Then your airtight plan won't work, will it?"

"Don't you worry about that. We will . . ." Sina hesitated, "make sure our man goes down. There are procedures for that."

"An innocent man dies in Iraq for you and everybody lives happily ever after?"

Sina squatted next to Malek. He grabbed both of Malek's wrists and forced him to meet his gaze. "There won't be any innocence to the guy who takes the fall for me, I promise you that. You have to believe me. Look at me. I'm Sina. Your friend. I found your mother. After thirty years I found her. I did this for you. For us. I'm not a stranger. All right?"

"What if James McGreivy doesn't pass on the information?"

"Then you have to convince him he should."

Maman was asking, "So you found the Afghan?"

"I did." Malek handed Maman five hundred-dollar bills.

She considered the American money and stuffed it in the folds of her *chador* where she kept little packets of heroin for customers. "God always protect you, son. What in return?"

He gave her Sina's address. "It's down the road from

here. You hear and see everything. If you think something bad will happen to him . . ."

"The Afghan cannot help him?"

"The Afghan is a guest in our country. There are risks he cannot take."

"Upon my eyes then. I pray to see you on satellite television."

"Maman, pray that you don't." He kissed her hand and walked off.

Babur sat waiting for him in a car two streets away from the park.

"Aqa Reza, your mother is a fine lady."

"Thanks for the grave. You got Anna's last name wrong, but it doesn't matter. My mother is happy about it."

"My apologies. God is great. One name is as good as another."

"If you say so. Can you get her out of the country on short notice?"

"I already said it: consider it done."

They were silent for several minutes. Babur drove until they fell into the expressway heading north. It was an unusually clear day and you could see the Elburz Mountains in all their majesty to the north of Tehran. On a day like this everything seemed possible. But it was a dream and Malek knew it. His body was switched off because of last night's opium. He was sure Maman could do little for Sina if and when it came down to it. He had really only given her the money because he wanted to.

He said to Babur, "Stay away from our mutual friend. He's trouble for you."

"Thank you for understanding that, Aqa Reza. I would help him slip away if you insisted. I am glad you do not insist."

"There is nowhere for him to slip to. He's like a fish in a barrel."

"What happened to him?" When Malek didn't respond, Babur answered himself: "I know what happened to him. He lost his way just a little more than the rest of us. I've known men like him. I saw plenty of them when I cooked in the camps back in those days."

Sina had given him the key to his motorbike and told him to take it out from the back of the teahouse by his old apartment. "I've been ordered not to go anywhere on my bike anymore. I guess they're afraid I might get lost or something. So my wheels are yours." When Malek came to fetch the thing, the teahouse owner wasn't there and his young assistant had to help him push the dormant bike until it coughed into a start. Malek rode for a long time after that. When it suddenly began to rain hard, he saw that all the bike messengers were huddled beneath the underpasses in the freeway waiting for the downpour to pass. He kept riding, willing the wet and cold to knock the dregs of opium out of his system. Then, at a less crowded underpass, he finally stopped and took out his phone.

James McGreivy answered.

"That thing I told you about . . . about my friend, it's more serious than I thought."

It was morning over there, East Coast time, domestic life in all its glory and tedium. He thought of another kid in one of the classes he'd taught the year before. Another vet farmboy from eastern Iowa who had ended up in Army counterintel, working out of Kuwait. In one of his class writing assignments for Malek he'd written that at nineteen he'd been saddled with assessing Lebanese men searching for work in Iraq. The kid's task was to see whether or not any of the Arab job seekers were Hezbollah moles sent there by the Iranians. He had written about it all with humor and a level of self-deprecation and humility. No post-traumatic stress disorder on this guy. He was more like Babur, able to adjust and move on. How was it some people could do that and others couldn't? Was it always just a toss of the dice?

"What?" he heard James shout.

Malek hung up the phone.

Around dusk, when he finally locked the bike in front of Soaad's building and went up, there was a surprise guest waiting for him in the kitchen.

The two women seemed to have hit it off.

Soaad pointed to Sina's mother. "Azar *khanum* has been here since noon. Where have you been? Where were you last night?"

There was just a slight tinge of motherly crossness in Soaad's voice, as if Malek were still the kid she would haul to her old Communist poetry meetings.

Malek bowed slightly to Sina's mother and stood at the kitchen door while the two women sat at the table sharing tea and biscuits. He wondered if Azar would notice Sina's bike parked out there on the street. Or if she would even care. The scene of his mother and Sina's mother sitting there in the kitchen made him uncomfortable. He had given Soaad's telephone number to

Azar just in case, but never figured she'd actually show up here. It breached some sort of protocol to Malek's mind, though he wasn't sure what.

Azar said, "Reza *jaan*, I have come to ask if you know where my son is."

"I know where he is."

No more was said, but his answer now brought intermittent weeping in that kitchen. First it was Azar who, Malek guessed, was crying from relief. Soon, Soaad joined the other woman in tearing up quietly. They were both graceful about it. None of that wailing of Middle Eastern mothers. Though it tore at Malek just the same. And a few minutes later he found himself back on the street calling Fani, telling him they had to meet right away.

Within a half hour they were in a basement pool hall around the corner at Ferdowsi Square. Billiards had been banned during the revolution and only in recent years did they allow the pool halls to reopen. This particular place was bare-bones ragged, the kind of joint only small-time drug dealers and washed-out pool sharks hung around in, waiting for innocents to drop by. They were men with desperate faces who had known cheap, plentiful liquor and entire city blocks of brothels before 1979. The first two decades of the Islamic Revolution had been particularly unkind to a lot of these men, and only in the past several years had they managed to burrow out of their hideouts.

Fani went to the back and told the errand boy to bring him a sandwich. Then he asked Malek, "What is it?"

"Sina's mother is at my mother's house right now."

"Should I be curious about that?"

"Not particularly. I'm actually here with a demand."

Fani laughed. "Let's hear it."

"First this: I've signed all the papers you wanted me to. You're getting your money—and I've found Sina."

"Oh?"

"Let me finish. Tomorrow, you and I will go to the judge and you'll ask him to release that small parcel of land that belongs to Sina's mother. It's her right. You'll let that one property go."

"That would not be in my interest. But fair enough, supposing I do that?"

"Then everything you and your bosses get from Sina's estate, it's yours. You can tell every *hajj aqa* you work for that I want nothing for my signatures. No commission. Nothing. I just want to gather my own mother and take her away from this city. And for that I will need a passport. Only you can provide her with that. So it's a guarantee I won't betray you. I won't go back on what I've signed."

"Malek, have you developed an interest in saving all the mothers of the world?"

"I'm only interested in saving two of those mothers. What do you say?"

Fani sighed, but it seemed genuine to Malek. "Look, I am reasonable. And because I am reasonable, we have a deal. This might get me in trouble with my, as you say, *hajj aqas*, but you can tell that woman she can go to court the day after tomorrow. That should give me enough time to fix it. The land will be released to her and she can sell it whenever she wants and to whoever she wants. Her financial worries are over. Now . . . tell me about your friend. I am impressed that you managed to find him."

"Don't play—you already know where he is."

"I have no reason to lie. I don't know where he is. Mine is strictly a financial affair with Sina Vafa. If I go looking for him too hard or seem too interested in his person, I may find myself burdened with the people he has worked for. Those fellows do not take kindly to having someone seek out one of their own. Especially the ones in current disfavor."

"Then why show me those videos of the American contract workers?"

"Because, as I said, I don't want him to become a martyr. I need this person alive. For now."

"Then the two of you see eye to eye. Like I told you before, he doesn't want to die either. I believe Sina had those on his computer intentionally. He wanted you to find them."

Malek watched Fani's face. The man's eyebrows were creased and he was thinking hard, wondering if all of a sudden it was he who had become Sina Vafa's plaything. Malek could see the seasoned operator considering all this and dismissing the possibilities one by one from his mind. Finally he said, "In that case, I am glad that your friend and I understand each other."

The errand boy returned with Fani's sandwich, which he ate fast, taking enormous chunkfuls with each bite. Malek continued observing him. Shadowy men lurked on the other end of the basement hall, glancing from time to time at the strangers, trying to size up Malek and Fani. One of the more courageous men eventually sauntered over and asked if either of them wanted a game. Fani dismissed him with a wave of the hand and the guy, thin as one of those old pool sticks, shuffled like a drugged animal back to his own game.

Fani washed down the last of his chicken sandwich with orange soda. "I'm not a monster, you know. But I have to protect myself. That woman, Sina's mother, may keep the piece of land. You got my word. I won't change my mind again."

"Why did you change it the first time?"

"I already told you why. Everything about Sina Vafa told me he'd be ready to die once he was guilt-free over his mother."

"You expect me to believe this cheap psychology?"

Fani sighed again. "Look, Malek! Tehran is not your America. This town I live in, every day the laws change. The guy who is king today ends up in a prison cell to-morrow. One man is disgraced, another has to confess to crimes he never committed, and a third has to sell his soul. It is really quite simple: I don't even trust my own brother. Let alone anybody else. But tonight, here in this awful little nowhere, I've decided to trust you because I *know* you are not lying to me. How do I know? I know because there is nothing for you to lie about. This is the difference between us. I have a thousand things to lie about in this city. And you have nothing to lie about. So I trust you more than I trust myself." He extended his hand, grabbed Malek's, and shook it. "But I must insist again, and I mean it—this is not a joke to be taken lightly: if the Americans ever do come to Tehran with their tanks and soldiers, please do not forget to tell them I'm one of the good guys. I know you'll be at the front line inter-preting for them. So please put in a good word for your old friend Fani. And now you can leave. I will see you here this summer. And *you*, as well, please don't die on me either until our business is finished. I still need that last set of signatures for the sale proceedings."

Back at Soaad's, the two women were watching television in the kitchen. It was one of those dubbed Korean historical soap operas with a lot of angry swordsmen and kings glaring at one another. Both women sat with impassive faces, more blanked-out and dazed-looking than really paying attention to the show.

Soaad said, "Azar has a request."

Malek went to the TV and turned it off, then joined the women at the table. "How is your husband?" he asked Azar.

"He is unwell. We worked very hard for that property. You saw for yourself what the judge did the other day. We have nothing to live on. We are finished."

Malek had never made as much money as he'd been making during the past couple of years of teaching. All that good old American money and no one and nothing, except Soaad, to spend it on. How odd that if the Americans hadn't gone to war, Malek would have never written his book or gotten his academic job. He really owed his good fortune to the United States Department of Defense!

He reached into his pocket and brought out more hundred-dollar bills. He spoke English to Azar, maybe to diminish the awkwardness of the situation by using a different language. "Madam, please consider this a short-term loan until things improve for you." Her pride, he could see, was choking her. So he added quickly, "In two days we will return to that judge. I have word you will get your land. You can tell your husband."

He stood up to walk away before she could make a demonstration of refusing the money.

"My son is truly all right?"

"He sends his love."

Clara Vikingstad's two bodyguards, the ones he'd stood shoulder to shoulder with last summer during that fight in Qum, caught up with him outside the courthouse.

Malek was feeling good. It was the satisfaction of having done something concrete. He had just taken Azar and her husband into the room of the same judge who had completely brushed the three of them off the previous week. But this time around the judge, a minor government attorney with slightly crazy eyes, was the model of propriety. He nervously explained that there had been a trivial mistake in the documents presented to him before, then ordered his servant to prepare tea. Azar and Afshar sat in the same seats as last week looking on in disbelief. Was it possible?

In the corridors of the courthouse, badly dressed men shuffled back and forth carrying papers and briefcases. There was an air of languid nothingness about it all, like this was all make-believe. But it wasn't make-believe. It only took three signatures, copied four times over, for the property to be transferred to Sina's mother's name. The last signature, and the most important, was from Malek, Sina's representative. When it was all done and the parties finished the final exchanges of goodwill and left the room, Malek reentered the judge's chamber and met the fellow's roving eyes. "For your troubles." He left a thick envelope full of money on the desk. The judge, for the sake of saying something, remonstrated that the Persian new year wasn't for another two months. To which Malek replied, "The new year comes early with your fine deed, *hajj aqa*."

Azar and Afshar waited in the hall until Malek returned. "How can we repay you?" Afshar asked, still seeming a bit dazed from what had just happened.

"This land is really and truly yours now. But do sell it fast. They can always change their minds."

Afshar started to say something, but his wife cut him off. "God protect you." She tugged at her husband to leave, but lingered for another moment. She met Malek's eyes. "God protect you," she whispered again, and pulled her husband after her.

Malek walked down the steps of the courthouse, where he found Clara's bodyguards waiting for him. The two men seemed genuinely glad to see him again and joked about his life in America.

Malek finally asked, "Am I in trouble, brothers?"

"Not today."

And that was all either of them said about why they had come after him. They appeared almost too carefree. Which usually spelled some kind of trouble. Malek then settled into the backseat and let the men take him to their boss's house.

He sat waiting in the same receiving hall he'd met Clara in half a year ago. When The Man finally came in, Malek was struck by how tall he was. He appeared distinguished and relaxed. The papers always described him as a politician of too few words. His thick white hair was parted to the side and once in a while he would run a hand over it as if to make sure it was all still there. Just that morning Malek had glimpsed a picture of him in a rival newspaper. The accusations were heating up and The Man and his team were blamed for plotting antirevolutionary shenanigans to disturb the upcoming summer elections.

"I am glad I was informed you are in town, Mr. Malek. I have something I want you to relay to Miss Clara."

"Forgive my words, but can you not pick up a phone and call her yourself?" Malek asked in the politest tone he could muster.

"It is not a good time to communicate directly. It is, in fact, a bad time. This is why I sent for you."

Several random thoughts went through Malek's head: One, could this guy steamroll over the establishment and get a passport for Soaad? Two, just how many people had he executed during the darkest days of the revolution? And did he have nightmares about that time? And did turning into a "reformed" revolutionary mean that you were absolved of past sins? Was it all so simple?

"I will be happy to relay any messages you have. Your wish is my command."

The politician turned away, as if searching for a sign on the walls of this enormous room studded with poor choices of glitzy furniture. "I want you to tell Clara *khanum* not to come here for the election." The muscles on the man's face tensed up as he spoke. It was almost impossible to imagine this. The man's career was one of solely getting ahead. Guys like him had confiscated the homes of men like Sina's father during the revolution before later selling them and putting the money in their own pockets. They'd taken over businesses, taken cuts in oil deals and mining operations. They had the power to send freighters filled with weapons to Damascus and South Beirut. They had the run of the place. So why the anxiety? It was like a page had been torn out of an otherwise perfect playbook.

"Just have them deny her a visa, *hajj aqa*," Malek said. "If she can't gain entry to the country she can't be here for the election."

"I have no power over that now. My enemies have given her the visa already. They want her here."

"And if she comes, you cannot guarantee you can protect her. That's what you're saying?"

He nodded. Yes, that was what he was saying. It was a bad time, he said. A very bad time. It came down to the simple fact that he knew something no one else wanted to believe right now: the election was going to be a fraud. His enemies were going to win; they would probably start putting a lot of people in jail. He didn't say that he himself would be one of those people, but the intimation was clear. All his life he had been wise enough to hedge his bets, but now the great man—the jailer of so many opposition fighters and one of the revolutionary student leaders who had stormed the American embassy and taken hostages—found himself cornered. Cornered, but at least clever enough to realize it. His gang would lose the election. And once they did, he would go down. He didn't want Clara here. Why? *Because*, Malek thought, *this son of a bitch is in love*. In love with Clara Vikingstad! He is so in love with her that he's willing to call me here to relay a message. *Don't come, Clara, they'll get you!* This man who had burned more than his share of American flags was now in love with an American reporter and would do anything to protect her. If Malek had the guts, he would have asked, *So, did storming the American embassy in 1979 and storming Clara Vikingstad in 2008 give you the same pleasure,* hajj aqa?

"*Hajj aqa,*" Malek instead said, "I will deliver your message to Clara *khanum* in person. You can rest assured I will carry the message."

NEW YORK CITY

Soaad called almost every day. He had instructed her not to say anything of substance over the phone, so she mostly talked about missing him. They had settled into a familiar mother-son relationship that revolved around her asking if he ate well and got enough sleep. There was something both ridiculous in this and also reassuring. His last day in Tehran, she had insisted on coming to the airport with him. After seeing off his luggage, they had stood on opposite sides of the departures hall glass divider and looked at each other like they were each being sent into exile. As if this was it and there would never be another chance to be together again. It made him think of borders that could never be recrossed and, in turn, of Anna. One day Soaad had asked him, "Where was that town Anna was born in?"

"Does it really matter now where she was born?"

Yes, it did. She wanted to go there. She wanted to see what Anna had left behind.

"You really wish to do that?"

He had to understand, Soaad explained, Anna was all she had for so many years. "What if I lost you tomorrow, Rez? It would be the same. Anna and I, it was like we were two people stranded on some island. I owe her something."

So he'd promised her Poland. Of all the places in the

world, he had pledged to take her to Poland to "experience" Anna, and then to Fresno, California, so she could visit Malek's father's grave too.

Meanwhile, he put off the two tasks he'd been charged with back in Tehran. He avoided James and didn't call Clara. Then, in the third week of February, there was a bombshell. James had written something online about his misadventures as a former Marine trying to work in academia. He wrote of carefree incompetence in the civilian world and contrasted it with the hard, crystal-clear reality of military life. In no time Malek got a call from the department head to come see him.

It was a planned attack. At the university, Malek walked quietly next to the department head into the office of one of the higher-ups where two men and one woman, none of whom he'd ever seen before, were waiting for him. The two men had almost identical ponytails and were both stocky, their expensive suits seemingly ready to pop open on them. And in their eyes, behind the reflections of their glasses, Malek could sense that they had been discussing him until the moment he walked through that door. The woman sat a little farther to the side. She had a small round head and was carefully dressed, an aging and precise administrator. It was the world of bureaucrats in this room, not professors. But they appeared friendly enough. Offered him coffee and asked him to sit in a comfortable chair.

Still, something about the setup reminded Malek of the times he had been "invited" to the Intelligence Ministry in Tehran to see if he would cooperate with them. He also glimpsed a printed copy of James's article sitting on the desk. He imagined one of those two ponytailed men was the boss, but could barely tell them apart, leaving Malek to wonder which of them had the real power in that room.

The department head explained to the others who Malek was, what an "excellent" job he had been doing the past two years at the college, and that they hoped to keep him here if they could come to some kind of understanding.

The understanding was that they wanted James Mc-Greivy gone. They didn't say it in so many words, but it was there, the unspoken elephant in the room which they had to get to sooner or later.

The woman and one of the two men remained quiet for a while and it soon became apparent to Malek that the other ponytail was the fellow to reckon with. They asked him if he liked the university. He said yes. They asked if he wanted to continue here. Yes. Did he like his students? Very much. Yes and yes.

At last, the boss lifted James's article from his desk and began: "You are a colleague of Mr. McGreivy." It was a statement and Malek nodded in assent. "How well do you know Mr. McGreivy?"

"I know him somewhat."

"I assume you have read this article."

"It would have been hard to avoid it around here."

"What do you think of it?"

"It's one man's take on what happens in a workplace."

"Do you agree with it?"

He felt hot. Not out of anxiety but anger. They had decided to cajole and browbeat him at the same time. Which was why three of them plus the department head were in this room right now. Just one of these people would have been enough. But they wanted results. They wanted James out. Yet Malek, a fixer from the battlegrounds of the Middle East, could already smell their questions coming a mile away. They were tough people, but tough only for a safely insulated place like this.

"Sir," he said with just enough cool to bite the edge off the tension in his throat, "what I think about McGreivy's article is my business. Please tell me why I'm here."

The room went silent. One of the ponytails stared hard at him but did not appear particularly displeased, just maybe a little surprised. The others glanced at their shoes for a moment. Malek took all this in. And suddenly he felt the familiar protectiveness for McGreivy and Sina and Soaad. He wasn't going to let anyone bully them. Or bully him, for that matter.

"Late last semester," the woman said, "there was an incident in front of the school gym." She had an excessively soothing voice like an elementary school teacher's. "You happened to be the victim of an attack by a man who, we have come to find out, was recently out of prison. From what we've gleaned of the campus security report and other sources, we've concluded that this was a case of mistaken identity. You were attacked by a man who mistook you for James McGreivy. It was James McGreivy that he was after."

She stopped and eyed him for a response. They were all examining him curiously. Malek gave nothing away. He stared straight back at the woman, and realized she must be some kind of a lawyer for the school.

"That incident is in the past for me. I have nothing against the man who hit me."

"That is not the issue," the woman said.

Standing his ground, Malek raised his voice just slightly: "Let's hear the issue then."

There was another pause. Now one of the ponytails spoke again: "Do you know a student named Candace Vincent?"

"She was my student and she was there when I was knocked down. You already know all this."

"Mr. McGreivy is having an open relationship with this student on our campus."

"Candace Vincent is thirty years old. She is not James McGreivy's student and never has been that I know of. And she has two kids already. So I don't see how it's any of my business what they do with each other on their own time."

Malek saw the department head squirming in his chair. He was sitting next to Malek, facing the other three. After a few seconds went by in silence, the department head said in his high, nasal voice, "I called you in here today for a good reason. Indeed, Mr. McGreivy is openly living with a student of ours. He has been holding some kind of strange self-defense course at the gym—which, by the way, we have put a stop to—where nearly all the students are women. He has called into question time and again the honor of our department, and now . . . now he has gone and written this article making us a laughingstock. So it would behoove you—"

Malek stayed focused on the three people in front of him, but interrupted the department head's diatribe. "Behoove me? I'll tell you what the issue is: you guys are sick and tired of McGreivy. And to be honest, I can't say I blame you too much. James McGreivy can be a hard-headed man."

"Now we're getting somewhere," one of the ponytails chimed in.

"But I'm not going to help anyone bring a case against
him. I'm not going to sue anybody because someone
knocked me down. I have no problem with whomever
Mr. McGreivy chooses to sleep with. And as for this
stupid article he's written, people write this stuff every day. With all due respect, I think you are upsetting
yourselves over a dead issue. You won't be renewing
McGreivy's contract for next year and he won't be wanting to come back either. If you try to give him a hard
time, he'll fight you. Why? Because he's a trained fighter.
You want to punish him and you've called me here today
to help you do that. In return, what do I get? A guarantee of a permanent job. Who wouldn't want that! But I
won't do it at James McGreivy's expense. He's served
his country well—"

The same ponytail laughed now. "Mr. Malek, he
served in a war you've criticized in your own writing."

"That doesn't mean he didn't serve well, sir! I saw
plenty of men like him in Iraq. Some of them were pieces
of shit. But a lot of them, they were men I would take a
bullet for."

The woman smiled. "You'd take a bullet for Mr.
McGreivy?"

"Madam, I didn't see the likes of any of you in Baghdad taking bullets for your country, did I?"

"What does that mean?"

Malek was spent. He didn't want to flail at these
people. But they'd forced him into it.

"It means . . . even if the world's gone to hell, honor
still matters. And a guy like McGreivy, he's an honorable

man. He's honorable now, and he was honorable when he was commanding house-to-house in Fallujah." Malek saw that he had drawn a blank from them on mentioning Fallujah. He settled back into his chair and exhaled. "Look, let's just be wise about this."

Ten minutes later, when he finally left that room, alone, peace had been reestablished. What he had said to them about James McGreivy being a fighter seemed to have sunk in. They had collectively seen the error of their ways. If they tried to mess with the former Marine he would bring their whole house down. On the other hand, if they stayed quiet, another three months and the guy would be out of their hair altogether. They might get a little flak because of the article, but it wasn't the end of the world.

Yet Malek realized that after a meeting like this, he himself might have to take one of those think tank jobs in Washington after all. Meanwhile, Clara had finally called a few days ago and left a message saying the end run to the elections in Tehran seemed to be getting hot and that he should be ready to fly with her in early June. He hadn't returned her call yet. But she was going to be in New York giving one of those I'm-a-war-correspondent lectures soon. It would be at the Midtown library and he'd catch up with her there to relay her protector's advice in person.

The next day, Malek stopped briefly in the mailroom of the English office to pick up his mail. There was an envelope from the administration offices sitting in his box. He opened the letter. It said that they were happy to inform him that his contract at the college had been extended into the following year.

* * *

Malek walked north. After Trinity Cemetery he didn't turn onto his street, he just continued walking. He wasn't sure he would actually go there until he was smack in the middle of the 181st Street Bridge between Manhattan and the Bronx. Ahead of him lay the projects where Candace and her kids—and now James McGreivy—lived.

It was a Friday and neither Malek nor James had classes to teach that afternoon. Malek sat on a bench between the fences of two basketball courts. In one of the courts a game was on. A brisk February day, but not freezing. Young mothers pushed strollers on the asphalt. People eyed him suspiciously—a white guy sitting on the bench like that. Undercover?

"I'm down by your building."

"Get yourself up here, *hajji*. I could use a hand with this damn kitchen."

James had all the cabinets on the floor. There was sawdust everywhere and carpentry tools lay about. The place was one of those huge project apartments that you'd have to pay an arm and a leg for anywhere else in the city.

The walls in the rest of the house were freshly painted. The rooms clean. James gave him a tour and then popped open two beers.

"You've been hiding from me, Rez. Not answering my calls. How come?"

Malek had thought he would do it casually, reel out the info on Sina after maybe half a dozen drinks in some bar. But now it came out, because the sooner he got done with it the easier he'd feel.

"My friend that I told you about, he's . . ."

James was fussing with an Allen wrench set. They were both sitting on the floor in the only clean corner of the kitchen. He glanced up and caught Malek's eyes. "You have something you want to say to me about him?"

"He's going after American contract workers now."

"Shia sector?"

"No. Up north. Kirkuk. Kurdistan mostly."

"You came here to the Bronx to tell me this?"

"No, I came to tell you the suits just tried to railroad me at the college. It was about you."

James laughed, though the serious expression didn't leave him. "What do you want me to do, Rez?"

"About what? Your screwup at the college? Or about my friend in Iraq?"

"Let's start with the second."

"He has to be stopped."

"What do you care? There are hundreds like him. Thousands."

Malek thought, *I am sitting on this kitchen floor with James McGreivy pretending I'm having a crisis of conscience.* Pretending that he wanted Sina Vafa, his best friend, stopped at any cost. And at the same time he had to pretend it wasn't easy for him to do this. The intricacy to the web of half-lies made him sick. And it was no figurative sickness. He excused himself to the bathroom for a minute.

When he came out, James was standing in the hallway holding a handsaw. "You got some intel on your friend? Recent areas of operation. Contacts."

Malek nodded. Sina had worked all of that out with him. He asked, "What will you do?"

"I already did something."

"What?"

"I told someone."

"Who? The colonel, your father?" Malek asked, acting shocked. Though he wasn't. Not nearly.

"Maybe I *should* tell the colonel. He'll think of me as halfway back to being his patriotic son again."

"Who did you tell, James?"

"I couldn't go through official channels. They'd be knocking on your door tomorrow. I told it to a former colleague. A fellow doing postdoc now at the American University in Beirut. He happened to be in town for a seminar."

"He's what I think he is?"

"No. At least I don't believe so. But I'm pretty sure one night soon over some Lebanese wine on Hamra Street in Beirut he'll pass the intel to someone else. And that someone will pass it to someone else. It will find its way to where it needs to. These things have lives of their own. And if your information is legit . . ." McGreivy didn't finish his sentence.

"You told him where your information came from?"

"I told him I dreamed it, for all you should know. Look, what do you care how I told him?"

Malek was now standing face-to-face with James. "But what if I'd made you promise not to tell anyone about this?"

"You didn't."

"But what if I had, James?"

"I would have still passed it on."

"Because your country comes first. Right?"

"Damn right!"

Malek turned to the door.

James asked where he was going. "You just got here."

He had to act hurt. He had accomplished exactly what Sina asked him to do. He had done it by default, and he had done it quickly. "Is that why you wrote that article about the college too? Because America needs fixing all over?"

"In that regard, me and my old man don't disagree too much."

Malek opened the door. "The college people, they were out for your blood. I convinced them to be patient."

"Thanks, friend. They won't have to see me again after this year."

"That's exactly what I told them too, and they bought it. But tell me: wherever you go after this, you're certain you'll take Candace with you?"

"That I will."

"You'll do it for America? Or really for Candace?"

"For both. And there's nothing wrong with that." Malek began to leave. "Wish you'd stay, Rez. We'll have dinner out. Candace and the boys will be here soon."

Malek didn't turn around, but asked quietly, "Do you still need more intel on him?"

"Wouldn't hurt."

"I'll do what I can. But no pictures."

"Smart *hajji*. And thanks for not selling me out at school."

"I don't sell people out. I guess I'm not quite American enough for that yet."

"Aw, that hurts, Rez."

"It was meant to."

The large reception hall of the New York Public Library

was full of old, wealthy donors to the place. Clara Vi-kingstad was all smiles, but also serious. She was a crowd-pleaser who understood how to work her audi-ence. There was a moderator and a couple of other for-eign correspondents, but Clara was by far the toast of the evening. She talked about her profession with verve and knowingness. She spoke of the war, the soldiers she'd met, the terrorists she'd interviewed or almost in-terviewed. There were unspoken but closely hinted sug-gestions of life on the line, of pushing the boundaries of her job. She talked about her one-day incarceration in Tehran and about how she was heading there again soon to cover what promised to be an intriguing election.

When it was over, people clapped and headed out into the New York evening. The talk about war had evaporated so fast that it was as if it had never hap-pened. In fact, the war itself now felt more like window dressing than something real. Malek felt guilty for even being here and wondered what Soaad was doing right now in Tehran. He thought about the heroin dealer, Ma-man, sitting in that park all day in the far south of the city selling her goods from under her *chador*. And what of Sina? What was he up to just then? Was he still teaching the poor kids of his neighborhood the English alphabet?

When the hall had emptied out, Clara finally noticed him standing there. She was standing with the people she'd just been on stage with and a few cheery hangers-on. Her boyfriend was there too, the esteemed war photog-rapher with the thick résumé. He stayed put as Clara excused herself from the group and walked up to him.

"Rez. We're all going out for drinks. Why not come with us? We can talk then."

"I'm not equal to the company, Clara," he joked. "I can't sit across from you and your gentleman friend and not feel heartbroken."

"Oh, Rez. Come on!" She tried to drag him back with her.

He could see the photographer was glancing their way and pulled his hand out of hers. "Clara, I've come here as a messenger."

She stopped and looked at him intently. "From Tehran?"

"Yes. Your *friend*, he wanted me to tell you something."

"I've had no word from him for a while. Nothing. It's very strange."

"He called me in. Told me he could not communicate."

"Out with it then," she said impatiently.

"He says that you should not come to Tehran. He can't guarantee your safety."

"What?" She sounded outraged. "My book is riding on that trip. And there's the election."

"I'm just a courier, Clara."

"What exactly did he say? Tell me his exact words."

"His guys picked me up one day, took me to that place you were staying at last summer. He wanted you to know that things are not what they seem. His own position is shaky. He can't guarantee anything. He begs you to stay put. I believe he cares enough that he took the risk of telling me these things in person. He could have easily not done it. It says something about the man he is. Don't you think?"

"You are a fool, Malek."

He saw that Clara's little crowd was slowly coming their way. She may have saved him in Baghdad, but now she had insulted him. And maybe the only way to save her skin and keep her from doing something as stupid as returning to Tehran was to insult her back: "No, the fool is you, Clara. If you go to Tehran, best find yourself another interpreter."

"Fuck you, Malek."

"You already did, my dear. Remember? It was brief. And not always sweet. I guess it's just that way with us *hajjis*. Kind of like sleeping with your butler or something."

Clara did not call him again. Soaad rang in late April, and in a roundabout way let it be known that she had finally sold the house, as planned, to that "certain friend." There was excitement in her voice. She said that the friend had been generous and told her she had until the end of the summer before she had to vacate her place. "I'm selling a few things nowadays," she said cryptically, meaning her furniture, which wasn't much to begin with.

Until then, getting Soaad out of Tehran had seemed like a future dream. He had put all the wheels in motion for it to happen, but had never actually considered a specific date. Now that specific date was the end of summer. If Fani went back on his word, Malek would have to give the go-ahead to the Afghan. Get his mother out of the country illegally. Probably through Pakistan. But then what? Without an American visa, Soaad would be a refugee in a foreign country. Clara Vikingstad, he knew, had the State Department contacts to get the visa approval. But that was a bridge already burned. And even if Clara did that for him, where exactly would the

Americans stamp the visa for Soaad when she didn't even have an Iranian passport?

It was the typical catch-22 life of a refugee.

And that had been Anna's world. Maybe it was why his mother was so adamant about establishing a marker for her friend, a final place, even if that final place was bogus. Some intuitive understanding of two women from two different worlds who had ended up neighbors in the heart of Tehran.

As spring kicked in and the semester began to wind down, he thought more and more about Anna. She was like an unattended ghost whose story would have to forever lurk in the periphery of other more pressing stories. Lost in life, lost in death. So to pass the time he had left before going back to Tehran, Malek delved deeper into Poland. He tried to follow Anna's trail through other people's books. First those Siberian gulags, then Central Asia, then Tehran.

One day he found the book of a Holocaust writer who had compiled a report on Jews like Anna who'd ended up in Tehran. Malek called up the old survivor and visited him in DC where they had dinner together. He told Louis about Anna and her phony grave somewhere in Tehran, how she had been Malek's mother's neighbor for years and years, and how Malek's mother was alone now and he was trying to get her out of the country.

"I know something about needing to get out of a place," Louis said. And the two men went on to drink late into the evening until both of them were a little wasted and gloomy. Then Louis called Malek a cab to take him to Union Station to catch his train back to New York City.

The train ride itself brought Malek back to this time last year. That was when Sina had first beckoned him to Tehran. And he half expected that as the train passed through Delaware, his cell phone would ring again and there would be Sina asking when he was returning.

Sina!

Malek dared not ask James McGreivy what had become of the information he'd passed along. *I have blood on my hands* was what he had wanted to tell the old Holocaust writer. *I lie for a living, Louis. I lie to save my own mother. Did you have to lie like that back then in Poland when you were a child?*

Being in DC had also brought the temptation to call Clara. But for all he knew, she was already in Tehran by now. The news from there was exciting. The opposition had taken off and it seemed like reformers had real support. Malek could not argue with the images he saw on TV and what he read in the newspapers. So maybe Clara's man in Tehran had been mistaken. Maybe Clara was right and all was safe and good. Maybe he should be with Clara right now, interpreting for her again. Just like old times.

Candace Vincent was calling his name and knocking on his office door. "Professor! Looks like we need to feed you."

"How is the new life going, Candace?"

She looked different. Her braided wine-red hair had gotten longer, sexier. She was also leaner, more muscular, healthy. There was a shine in her eyes too that hadn't been there last year. *Joie de vivre*, Malek thought. That was the thing most different about her. She hadn't had it even half a year ago, but she definitely had it now.

"How come you never come see us?"

"I did. About a month ago. But you and the kids weren't there."

"You think what I got with your friend is bad for him?"

She was still standing up. He asked her to shut the door behind her and sit. Malek had covered the stuffy, windowless room with Indian fabrics to make it a little less claustrophobic. He watched her take her boots off and sit on the Persian rug he'd laid on the floor. She hugged her knees and stared at him, waiting for an answer.

"I'll be honest, it's not my business," he said.

"Yeah it is. You're a part of my life. *Our* life. People pick and choose who to let in, who to keep out. It's like being part of a tribe, you know? I seen you take a bad blow that day from my kids' pops. And what do you do? You sit there, say nothing, give no one away. How come? 'Cause you one of us. Me, you, Jimmy—we the same people. Different skin, different hats. But the same people."

"Okay."

"Okay, what?"

"Okay, don't be angry with me. And I do think you are good for James. And he for you."

"Good. 'Cause Jimmy said you avoiding him and you got your reasons and we gotta respect those reasons. And that's all right with me. I don't mind it. But, you know, we leaving here in a few weeks. Jimmy's taking us to the West Coast. There's no job lined up, but he says that'll come. It always does. I'm only here to ask if you'll have dinner with us just once. School ends next week. I'm graduating. I thought these fools would give me a hard time about what happened to you. But they didn't. Jimmy says they tried to give you a hard time though. But you were a true friend. You didn't budge."

"What happened to your kids' father?"

"Gone."

"Just like that?"

"What do you think life is, professor? All clear-cut cause and effect? It ain't. Sometimes shit just happens, you know? And then shit disappears, just plain goes away. Fella who hit you, he's not a bad man. I told you that before. He's just confused. And now his confusion took him elsewhere. I went to school four years in this place, just about got my degree now, and I can talk ghetto if I want to or I can walk into a job interview and talk like a princess, not forgetting my punctuation and grammar. My horizons, as they say, expanded. I can use words like *quintessential* and know what the hell I'm talking about. I can say *apropos* and my next door neighbor, God bless her, will look at me all bug-eyed thinking I come from another planet. My horizon did expand, professor. It did in all kinds of ways, not just in words. And James—Jimmy—he's a big, huge part of that expansion. And I got you to thank for it. So I'm here today thanking you, goddamnit!"

"You can call me Rez."

"Rez then. Won't you come have dinner with us just once before we all go our separate ways?"

"I will for sure."

So they were leaving for the West Coast and he was headed back to Tehran in another two weeks. He had actually run into James a few times at school. But a thickness had set in. An element of distance. It came from their secret. Sina Vafa sat between them like a crime they shared. And protocol said that neither should broach the subject anymore. Malek had done his part and James McGreivy had apparently done his. The rest was, well, in God's hands—God and the United States Army in Iraq.

These thoughts made him lonely. Which was why he hung on to Soaad more and more. And lately he had begun to have an irrational fear that something bad would happen to her. Now it was he who called her every day. The streets of Tehran, news kept showing, had turned into a carnival of preelection fanfare. There were celebrations and fights and marches and armed militias. Clara was there reporting officially now and she seemed fine. He'd already seen a couple of her reports. They were full of optimism, talking about "winds of change." It surprised him. She was seasoned enough to know better. Change always carried a price. Often that price was that there would be no change at all.

"Professor . . . Rez, you look like your head's in the clouds."

Malek's drifting gaze returned to Candace and he mumbled, "You and James, you guys are not just good for each other. You're a miracle. I'm deeply happy for you."

Candace peered down for a moment, saying nothing. When she spoke again it was in a quieter voice. "But I came to tell you this too: every night Jimmy wakes up sweating. Got them nightmares. It's not like these things they say about soldiers. It's not stress and all that. It's not like he drinks himself to sleep every night and needs a bunch of pills to stay standing during the day. None of that. I've been reading books about the soldiers having a hard time. James ain't having a hard time. Know why? Because James been having a hard time all his life. He's just a hard-time kinda man. You think some other woman could have understood and stood by him? I don't think so. No."

"You don't have to explain why you guys are good together, Candace. I already know you're good together."

"But I want to explain something," she insisted, raising her voice slightly.

He was sitting on a chair at his desk staring down at her on the floor. At that moment Malek saw something distinct in Candace Vincent's face: love. James McGreivy had found complete love. So much so that he could paint an apartment, redo its kitchen cabinets, and just two months later take his family and leave the place for good. He wanted them to live calm, beautiful lives at every moment of every day. James McGreivy, for all the night sweats and the boos from some of those former colleagues, was going to have a damn good life. James McGreivy was no casualty of Iraq.

"Jimmy and me, we understand each other, Rez. That's what it comes down to. *Understanding*. He won't have that with no one out there in Long Island, you know? And I sure as hell didn't find it in the hood. You know what I mean, right?"

"I swear to you, Candace, I know exactly what you mean."

So he went to their dinner. More like an afternoon get-together. He met Candace's boys for the first time. They were polite and looked up to James in a way that they might not have if they were a few years older. But at their age, the possibility that some white guy might suddenly parachute into their lives and stay did not appear beyond reason. They'd all caught each other at the right time. They were lucky that way.

Before dinner, they all went out to the courts. Malek, a stranger to basketball, sat beside Candace and they watched James and the boys. Soon there was a pickup game with neighbors and the kids went to another half-court to play by themselves. James gave as good as he got, his moves smooth and athletic. He high-fived with the other players and slowly, as the afternoon wore on, even his lingo switched ever so imperceptibly and blended into the courts. It was like he was wearing camouflage and disappearing into his surroundings. When he wanted to, McGreivy could become a part of the landscape.

At their job at the college he hadn't wanted to be a part of the landscape.

Malek caught a glimpse of Candace looking on with satisfaction at the game. Then she turned Malek's way and smiled, as if to say, *Didn't I tell you?*

After dinner, James walked Malek to the other side of the bridge.

"I'll drive you to the airport tomorrow if you like."

"No."

"I doubt we'll be here by the time you get back."

"I'll find you in California then."

James grabbed Malek's arm and they stopped just short of Amsterdam Avenue.

"I don't know anything more about your friend's fate, if that's what you've been wondering."

"I guess if I go to Tehran tomorrow and see him alive and well, then he's alive and well."

"And if not?"

"James, I came to you with this thing. It's not your war anymore. Go live your life in California. Get that beautiful woman and her kids out of the Bronx."

"You too. Get your mother out of that country."

It was a serviceable goodbye. Manly. Even the 181st Street Bridge looked more solid in the springtime as two fire trucks screamed across it.

And it was not until four blocks later that James caught up with Malek again, calling out his name.

Malek turned around.

"If they take your friend, won't it be trouble for you? I don't mean trouble here, but over there. Won't somebody in Tehran guess where the intelligence might have come from?"

James's eyes were on him. They were standing beside a Dominican barbershop blaring loud music.

There was nothing he could have said that wouldn't sound like a clumsy lie. So he offered the only response that at least had a grain of truth to it: "Just trust me!"

James looked surprised. "Trust you?"

"Yeah. That's all I ask."

TEHRAN

The world had changed.

Malek watched as Soaad, breathless and happy, insisted it was their duty to stay with the demonstrators as they made their way toward the university. The crowd took up nearly the entire length of Revolution Avenue. He couldn't tell how many there were. Tens of thousands? A million? He didn't care. He didn't want to be there. He hadn't come to Tehran to go to street demonstrations.

It was the third demonstration they'd been to together, with Malek only participating to make sure Soaad didn't get hurt. In the chaos of the days that had followed the election, he had not managed to get anything done. Fani was nowhere to be found, never answering his phone. Sina too was underground again. Down at his shack, the boy who ran the little shop for him claimed Sina had been gone since before the election.

Malek heard the rumbling of motorcycles before he saw them. The militiamen came in twos on the back of red motorbikes, armed to the teeth and wearing riot helmets and protective outfits that gave them an insect-like appearance. Somewhere near the Hafez Bridge, the throng that Malek and Soaad had been walking with was cut off from those just ahead of them.

Malek grabbed Soaad and broke for the shuttered shops on the north end of the sidewalk. The sticks were coming down hard on the demonstrators. Car alarms went off as windows were smashed. Yet there was something feline and precise about Soaad. She moved with the body of a woman less than half her age. And when Malek got a momentary glimpse of her face, there was not a trace of fear. She was excited and willing to fight. This made him even more protective of her. She was all he had. Even in that ruckus of teargas canisters and garbage dumps going up in flames, his mind registered that if he failed her now he would be failing everything.

A single file of three bikers came at them, and Malek's hand automatically went for a piece of loose brick lying at the foot of a knocked-over newspaper kiosk. The first two bikes went right past them. In that moment Malek caught the eyes of the stick-wielder riding on the back of the third bike, and knew that the man was getting ready to aim at them. At Soaad! Malek let the brick fly at the helmet of the one riding in front. The impact disoriented them just long enough for Malek and Soaad to hurry past the bridge and up Hafez Avenue.

It seemed a bit childish that they should be running like this, yet it felt like something that was long overdue and had to somehow be finished. Hadn't it been these very streets, only with different names, during the Islamic Revolution? Malek, who'd been thirty years younger, running down the same alleyways, minus Soaad, to get a good view of the crowds as the adults fought and sang revolutionary songs and sometimes got killed.

A yelp in the crowd not ten feet behind them brought everything to a standstill. A kid was bleeding badly.

Maybe from the bullet of a sniper. They heard the chants of *Allah Akbar* go up. But the motorcycles didn't stop. The batons kept coming. Then, in the melee that followed, Malek got separated from Soaad. A group of men were pushing him toward the motorcycles and soon fists and sticks were flying every which way and women were hugging the walls, screaming.

His clothes were torn but at least he had escaped without any bruises this time around. He stuck to the backstreets of downtown. People had improvised in their neighborhoods, bringing the injured in from the main thoroughfares and giving shelter to those being chased by police. As Malek passed each block, they saw his tattered clothes and offered him water. Some even offered him food and rest in their homes, telling him he should stay put until the roadblocks had been lifted.

All he wanted was to get home to Soaad.

A pall of smoke hung low over the city. Once in a while shots would ring out and echo through the narrow streets of downtown. People pointed and whispered about snipers on the rooftops of public buildings. It was such a different feel than the peaceful marches of just a week earlier. Now it was a free-for-all, like an end of something. How had it come to this? He tried calling Soaad's house, but the cell towers in the downtown area appeared cut off. He asked a family if he could use their landline to see if his mother had gotten home all right. They were gracious; they let him in and gave him tea. A little girl brought him a wet towel so he could cool his face.

Soaad didn't pick up. He thanked the family and

kept walking, not really knowing where he was headed. It was impossible to get anywhere near Ferdowsi Square to Soaad's apartment. They told him the whole area was cordoned off and police were hauling people into vans by the dozen.

Malek sat by a thin stream off a relatively quiet street. He had come to Tehran to sign a few more papers, fetch his mother, and leave. Maybe leave for good. But after the election went bad, people had finally taken to the streets. He'd thought it would be a passing thing. So he'd lingered, taking his time to call Fani. He had the whole summer, he figured. He'd watch the show. But then the show had turned violent. Whatever made him think it wouldn't? With time now on his hands, he had taken Soaad on another graveyard hunt. They'd visited cemeteries in the northeast of the country and in the south, where there had been other Polish camps during the war. It was like they were on holiday, mother and son—a Polish-cemetery holiday. And when they'd gotten back to Tehran the city was ready to go up in flames.

In the rivulet of water by Malek's feet, several plastic bags came together and quickly blocked the flow. Malek watched the murky liquid as it stabbed around the blockage.

His phone was vibrating. Surprised, he took it out, thinking Soaad had managed to reach him.

It was from the States. James.

"You all right there?"

"No."

"What's happening?"

"Blood. Bullets. Gas. Fire. Roadblocks. You know,

same old. Baghdad. Not nearly as bad, to tell you the truth. But bad enough."

"What the hell are you doing there, Rez?"

"You already know why I'm here."

"News here makes it sound terrible."

"News there always does. But you know better, captain. When you're in the thick of shit, it's never as awful. You get used to it. The smell. Everything."

"I've been trying to call you for hours."

Malek was too exhausted to give updates on how the street fights in Tehran were going. After a pause he asked, "Where are you, Jimmy?"

"Shoreline Drive. Santa Barbara, California."

"With the family?"

"Indeed. It's heaven here, Rez."

"I know it is. I surfed there for a whole week once. Ages ago. But just watch out you don't give the white folks there a heart attack with your family."

He heard James laughing. "I think I already did."

"Good."

"Anything else I should know, Rez?"

"Not yet."

"Well, you call if you need me."

"And you'll do what? Get a squad of Marine recons to come rescue me?" Now Malek laughed. "It's all right, my friend. Enjoy the Pacific Ocean. Nothing pacific about where I am."

"You call me, Rez, goddamnit."

"Will do, captain."

James McGreivy had become something of a pinup boy in Malek's head. Even when things were going badly for him, James always had two solid feet on the ground. He would raise his new family and maybe expand it. In time, he'd get his deadbeat brother and sister to move to California too, and he'd take care of them. He'd put everybody to work. He'd dutifully attend his father's funeral and afterward help his mother sell the house in Long Island and bring her to the West Coast to live downstairs from them. His mother would at first try to hide her shock of having black kids for grandchildren, but eventually she'd get used to it. James was a pinup poster boy, and a damn pretty one at that. He had a country to live for, and to die for if necessary.

Malek tried calling Soaad again. But, of course, the beautiful illogic that had just allowed him to talk to James in Santa Barbara, California, would not let him dial a number just half a mile away.

September 11 came back to him. *That* September 11. He'd been a graduate student then. Almost finished with his PhD thesis. He'd sat glued to the television in Austin, Texas, and when they showed people in New York crying after the Twin Towers fell, he had felt nothing. Wasn't true; he had felt something. It wasn't quite schadenfreude but something along the lines of, *Now you Americans too know what a burning building really feels like*. But wasn't he just another Sina Vafa? He wasn't out to get America. America had given him life, and now it was giving him a doctorate. He had never joined in those juvenile demonstrations in college like Sina had, and he had never, ever burned a US flag. But that day in September, for just a passing moment, he'd felt a charge of wicked euphoria that had quickly passed and in the days ahead turned into maddening guilt.

And now, sitting by this poor excuse for a stream in

Tehran and hearing the noises of death from less than a quarter-mile down the road, Malek recalled that day some eight years back and suddenly, out of nowhere, he began to weep. The crying lasted only about a minute, and when he was done he got up, shook himself off, and began walking toward Soaad's place. He didn't care if the police stopped him.

No one stopped him. He saw young men and women being dragged off by plainclothes thugs and thrown into prison vans. There were foot chases that brushed right by him, batons flailing. On the tops of balconies uniformed soldiers scoped targets. And still no one touched him.

Sometimes it was like that; you turned invisible. The sniper watched you from his window and knew you were not a target worth taking. So he shot the guy ten feet to your right in the stomach just because the man had an insolent grin on his face and needed to be disciplined.

He saw Sina's motorbike where he always parked it by Soaad's place. Burned, like a lot of bikes had been burned in the past week. The skeleton of the charred thing was on its side, half of it pushed underneath an unlucky car whose windows were shattered.

On the other side of the street two men sat in a small, brown, antiquated Renault. They were watching him. Low-level operatives. He knew the type. Their clean, inquisitive faces in the middle of that violent day, in that unlikely car, told him they were here for him.

Malek rang Soaad's buzzer and immediately the men jumped out of the Renault.

Soaad was buzzing him in.

Malek didn't move. When the men were close enough, he asked, "Who wants me?"

"Fani."

"Can I see my mother?"

"She is all right. She went in the building two hours ago."

"Would you gentlemen like some tea?"

One of the men shrugged and said okay. The other stared at his partner with disbelief. The one doing the shrugging said to the other, "Let him see his mother. Fani said not to push him."

Upstairs, Soaad had already set three glasses of tea on a tray and was waiting for Malek to take it down.

Malek observed his mother with some incredulity. She seemed to always be two steps ahead of him. "I'm sorry I lost you," he said to her.

She still bore that street-fighter look of a few hours ago. She came up to him and put her head on his chest. "I went somewhere today after we were separated."

"In this madness?"

"I went to your friend's mother's house."

"Sina's mother? Why?"

"I wanted to know she is all right." She backed off a step from his embrace. "They are not living there anymore."

"Maybe they moved away. Sold the place and sold the land I got back for them, then just moved to another town. Somewhere quiet and cheap."

"But what if something happened to them?" Her former political prisoner's mind was working overtime.

"It's not my business."

"It is."

"Soaad, I have two men waiting downstairs."

"Are they here about me?"

"No. They are not here for you."

"Can you get me out of this country?"

She asked it matter-of-factly, as if she were talking about a third person, not herself. She was used to such conversations—her life, like the lives of so many of her generation, was mostly an overture to escaping.

But now they had another problem. Babur, the Afghan, had disappeared. Malek had found this out during the first days he'd been back. In the roundups following the elections, the Afghan had taken a hit for doing what he did for a living. It wasn't the first time he'd had to go under and it wouldn't be the last. The men who worked for him assured Malek that Babur would be back by the end of summer once things calmed down in the capital. Malek had sat on this piece of information and didn't say anything about it to Soaad. It would have been more anxiousness over nothing. It was time, however, to share bad news. As he talked, they could hear the report of gunfire going off somewhere. Someone was getting killed around the corner. That was their reality. And Fani's guys were waiting downstairs for their damn tea.

Soaad asked, "Does Mr. Fani have a family?"

"All these sons of whores do. They are family men. Good family men. They go to picnics. They take holidays. They help their sons and daughters with their math homework. What do you suggest I do—appeal to his sense of being a family man?"

"Yes. That is what I suggest."

Malek drank his own tea in one swig and took the men's downstairs for them. They drank thirstily, as if all day they'd been waiting just for this. One of them took the tray and set it down by the door of the building. "Your mother will pick it up herself. Let's go."

For a second Malek watched the abandoned tray like he was leaving a part of himself behind that door. Then he followed the men to their car.

Clara Vikingstad was crying.

In the confusion of the last few weeks he had mostly forgotten about her. He'd known she hadn't escaped the city and was still filing her breathless reports. But as the demonstrations had gotten out of hand and the government began throwing foreign journalists out of the country, he'd just assumed they'd thrown her out too. At the same time he'd eventually stopped following outside news altogether. It was as if this new revolution on the streets of Tehran had created a cocoon where nothing that happened beyond it was of much use.

Which was why seeing Clara in that bare but brightly lit room completely discombobulated Malek. Something about this picture was wrong, but wrong not in the usual way that some journalist might be arrested for a short time. Clara was behind a steel table that was nailed to the floor. Her hands were cuffed in front of her. She wore an ugly gray uniform that sat like a shoe box over her, her head wrapped in the same grayness, giving her an archaic, nunlike look. She was thinned and colorless. She was in custody.

Malek sat across from her, as if he were an interrogator. The bright light invaded him and he could only imagine what it did to Clara. He tried to summon a measure of sympathy for her and was surprised at how little he could muster at that moment. Her ghostly look had none of the confidence and poise that she displayed in front of crowds. She was like a phantom. When he'd first been let into the room, she had been resting her head on the desk over her cuffed hands. She glanced up but said nothing. For a moment she stared at her own hands. Then she began crying.

"Clara," he called. Immediately she went silent, as if he'd barked at her instead of calling her name as softly as he could. "Clara," he repeated, even more quietly this time. Oh but that light! It ravaged him. Made him want to knock his own head against the horrible white wall.

"Rez," she barely brought out. It was the voice of a scared animal. The voice of someone who didn't know what their next few minutes would be like. "Rez, are you working for them?"

"Who?"

"The people who are keeping me."

"No, Clara. I work for nobody."

"Then why are you here, my love?"

My love? Now he was her *love*? He wondered if her famous war photographer friend had put out a search for her yet, or if the newspapers in the States had already begun a zingy chorus to get their world-class correspondent released from the clutches of Middle Eastern brutes.

"I told you not to come to Tehran, Clara. I brought you your special friend's warning. And do you know where your special friend is today?"

"I don't know where he is."

"He's in jail. A whole bunch of them are in jail. He and his friends lost the wager, Clara. They are arresting people like him left and right, shutting down their newspapers, leaning on their families . . . and you."

"What about me?"

"I don't know yet why they got you."

"Then why are you here?" She was staring at him. But her eyes were blank. Several times she seemed to nod out. She'd had little sleep. He could see that. He could also see she was warming to his presence. It brought relief. It gave her some kind of hope.

"I'm not sure yet why I'm here, Clara. But I'll know soon. How long have they been keeping you?"

She burst into tears again. She didn't know. She didn't know anything. She was losing her mind. *Rez, I am begging you, get me out of here.* They had kept her in a cell by herself. Not here though, she added. They'd brought her here only today. Sometimes there were sounds, like ghosts. Every day an old woman wearing a *chador* would come and stare at her for a few minutes. No interrogation. Just the old witch and her staring. Then she'd go away and a voice in bad English would announce from somewhere that Clara was going to be here forever. *No one knows where you are, Vikingstad.* The voice, a man's, said her last name as if the first *i* were two *e*'s instead: Veekingstad. She had lost track of time. She didn't know when it was night and when it was day. Sometimes she would hear laughter. Men laughing and that horrible old woman. "I can't do this, Rez. I can't stand it." She was moaning now. "I've done nothing. They won't even say what I've done."

He had to mention it: "Clara, I thought you said you

didn't mind being jailed for a couple of months. For your career's sake, I mean."

"You son of a bitch, Rez," she said weakly. "It's horrible. I can't do this. It's not for me. I don't know. Please! I beg you. You are not here for nothing. I don't know who you are. You are torturing me. Help me out of here, Rez. I'll do anything. Please!"

In the room next door, Fani waited for him. There were blowup photographs on the desk. A desk identical to the one that Clara was sitting at.

Malek picked up one of the photos: Soaad and himself and Anna in the Jewish cemetery of Tehran. Then another one of just Soaad and Malek at that other cemetery by the Caspian Sea.

"Not that I'm surprised," he said to Fani, "but why these photos?"

Fani was unusually disheveled and gave off the pungent smell of someone who hasn't showered for a few days. There were several other men of indistinct government variety in the building. They shuffled or lounged in the hallway, looking as bored and tired as traffic cops who had issued too many tickets.

Malek figured they must be close to 7-Tir Square, but he wasn't sure exactly where. The men he'd come there with had told him to drop his head to the floor of the car for the last few minutes of the ride and he'd done it automatically—wasn't the first time he'd been asked to do something like that. When he'd finally emerged from the car, they were in a basement parking lot and a half-lit neon sign blinked at the end of the driveway.

Fani scowled at him. "Sit!"

"Am I under arrest?"

"Don't be a fool."

"Why these photos then?"

"They collect things. It's their job. Photos especially. When they need to have something on you, they call you in, as I'm doing now, and they say, *Hello, Mr. Malek. How is your day? Take a look at these photographs, Mr. Malek. Tell us what you were doing in a Jewish cemetery. Do you work for somebody?* Then they will say, *And that woman, your mother, a known Communist with a jail term under her belt, what is she doing there with you and with that person of foreign origin?* They will ask these questions, and when you can't answer—which you can't, because there is no answer that is correct anyway—then they will draw a case against you. Sedition against the state. Spying for a foreign country. And so forth. Then you will object and say, *But I was just visiting a cemetery.* And they'll say, *Aha! But that's just it.* And you won't be able to argue. Because there is nothing to argue against. It's just you and these *incriminating* photos."

"What do you want?"

"One last signature."

"You want to embezzle everything from the Vafa estate. That's what this is about."

"It is not me, Malek. Take a look at where you are," Fani said wearily. "For all I know, this place," he gestured around the room, "might not even exist two days from now. Times are changing. Our streets have gone mad."

Malek finally understood what this was really about. Yes, it was about the Vafa estate. But it was also about a lot more. Fani was afraid. The men whose thumb he was under were afraid. The men at QAF who had been Sina's employers were afraid. But none of these people was sure what to be afraid about. Who was going to come out on top after these street fights were over? Overnight, all calculations had changed. And everybody wanted to claim their stake now, cash it in, and get out of Dodge if they could.

This still left the reality of Clara Vikingstad in that other room. Clara was just another blowup photograph, like the ones on this table. She was like a certificate of guarantee. To Fani, and to whoever Fani worked for, she was nothing but a bargaining chip. They would have to release her before things got too ugly. In the meantime, they could make a show that they meant business.

Malek watched as Fani pulled another file from his briefcase. On it was written *Orchid*, and Malek immediately presumed it was Soaad's dossier. Fani plopped the folder down and rifled through his briefcase before producing several more photographs. In one of them, Clara's gentleman friend who was now in jail was naked, and so was Clara. They were lying side by side, the man appearing to kiss Clara's back while she turned away, as if bored or disgruntled.

The other set of photos were of Malek and Clara. They went a few years back. Some from Tehran, but mostly taken in Iraq and Syria. In one photo Clara had a hand on Malek's shoulder, with a vague citadel-like edifice in the distance. It may have been Aleppo, but Malek wasn't sure. Not exactly a compromising photograph, but in a kangaroo court it could be made to signify anything. About that, Fani was completely right.

"You keep Clara Vikingstad any longer, there will be an international uproar."

Fani shrugged. "We like uproars."

"No you don't."

Fani leaned back in his chair. "Do you want to do business?"

"What have you done with Sina Vafa's mother and her husband?"

"Nothing that I know of. But I do happen to know they sold their place and moved away. I have an address for them."

Fani wasn't lying. He had no need to.

Malek finally sat down. "I'd like their address."

Fani nodded. "You seem to forget I was the one who originally gave his mother's number to you."

He had. It was true. And Malek wanted to ask why, but what difference did it make at this point? He waited for the other man to complete his maneuver. Fani took out more photos and spread them in front of Malek. They were pictures of a building that had been reduced to rubble.

Iraq.

"Your friend Sina Vafa was recently in Kirkuk for an operation."

"How do you know this, Fani?"

"Because I pay attention."

"Is he dead? Is he in that rubble?

"Don't play dumb, Malek. You know why he was there. You were a link in the chain of events that led the Americans to attack this building. But . . . oh so conveniently the building also happened to be a storage house for hundreds of pounds of ammunition that blew it all to ashes when the attack started. Whoever was in that building, his biggest body part is a toenail."

"And that toenail doesn't belong to Sina Vafa?"

"No, of course not."

"I won't ask you how you know these things. That's none of my business."

"Feel free to ask. I am here today to give you a lesson. You and me, Malek, we are nothing. We are faces. I thought I had bowed out and was working toward a comfortable retirement. But I guess I'm not. Our streets are in chaos and the Americans are not happy with us and all the *hajj aqas* uptown have passed the word down: *Call Fani and let him take care of it.* Because if things go bad tomorrow, they can say, *Look, it was all Fani's fault. It was Fani and that fellow Malek. They were working together. All the false signatures come from them.* You see, in the end none of us have much choice. Because once you start to play the game, your world doesn't expand; it gets smaller. Smaller and smaller. Your friend Sina knows something about that."

"Very nice speech."

"I have a dozen of these speeches."

"Why tell me about the Kirkuk operation?"

"So that with a relaxed heart you can stop protecting your friend. You can sign over your power of attorney without feeling guilty about it."

"I thought that my power of attorney cannot be transferred."

"Arrangements, my dear Malek, have been made. This is not the Tehran of last year. It is what they call an emergency situation."

Malek was numb. He didn't even have it in him to feel anger toward Sina. Fani was looking at him with eyes that maybe had some pity in them. The man pushed Soaad's file toward Malek. "I think you know what this is. Take it. Burn it." Malek opened the file. Several photos of Soaad, going back three decades. A beautiful woman. But also a fresh passport in there, with an up-to-date passport photo that had obviously been transferred and adjusted from Soaad's recent national ID card. Fani was giving him the green light to take Soaad out of the country. "These photos," Fani brushed a hand over the table, "we will throw them away. And that lady in the other room, she will be released before you can say the letter *aleph*."

"Doesn't it seem like overkill to even apprehend Vikingstad? You didn't need to do all this to make me sign over the Vafa estate to you."

"How many times have I told you that in Tehran our *friends* have calculations that go beyond our understanding. Miss Vikingstad is merely a means to an end. Somebody somewhere needed to be taught a lesson. And so Miss Vikingstad was brought in. It just happened that the arrest of Miss Vikingstad and our affairs, yours and mine, seemed to come together. And so here we are, at the end of the road."

"And Sina? Will you kill him, now that no one needs him?"

"What makes you think he is not needed anymore?"

"Once I give my last signature and his family estates are sold, he won't be of consequence."

Fani nodded resignedly, saying nothing.

"And that business in Kirkuk, it also closes the chapter on *something*. On what exactly?"

Fani sighed. "If they make me pay a visit to your friend, I will give you fair warning to start grieving."

"Why?"

"Because they will most probably put the blame on you eventually. And, come to think of it, on me. They will say we were his closest associates. I too am a replaceable man, Malek *jaan*."

Malek imagined living in a world without Sina. It didn't quite bring a lump to his throat. His friend was starting to become a newspaper story.

"To go that whole length just to destroy one Iraqi in Kirkuk!" Malek shook his head wearily.

"This is how you flush someone out while blaming his death on the good old Americans. It is a method. A way of thinking. They teach us these things in classrooms and we take notes and we apply our learning sooner or later. What we do is not cinema. It is tradecraft. It is real. All you have to do is go outside and run into the first roadblock down the street to be reminded of it."

"You and Sina's employers, you've reached an understanding then?"

"God is great."

Which of course meant yes, they had reached an understanding. Sina was, at last, completely expendable.

It was the end of the line.

"I'm ready to sign."

"Good. God is twice great. And I know of a notary who just happens to be open for our purpose on this very challenging day."

Malek stood up. "I need to see Vikingstad for one more minute."

"Oh, Malek, you are too sentimental. I have promised you she will be released."

"I want to tell her that she better get her contacts in the American State Department to issue a visa for my mother."

Fani opened his eyes wide. "Maybe she would do the same for poor Fani here?"

"Doubtful. But may I show this picture to her?" He pointed to the naked shot of Clara and The Man.

"Do you intend to blackmail her, dear Malek?"

"No, I just want to remind her not to write a book about all this, in case pictures like this one here might find their way to the wind."

Fani nodded with some appreciation. "You could always come back and work for us, Malek."

"I don't know who *us* is anymore." He took the photo. "I'll just be a minute."

On the flight back from Dubai, where they'd stamped her Iranian passport with an American visa, Soaad stared out the window at the clear blue expanse of the Persian Gulf, as if in a trance. And just once during the two-hour journey did she turn to Malek: "This is the first time I've gone abroad in my whole life."

"The other side of this gulf is not exactly abroad. Wait till we get to America."

"America!" she echoed, closing her eyes as if to imagine the place behind the name. "Why can't we just fly there now? Why must we go back to Tehran?"

"Unfinished business."

"Did you find your friend's mother?"

"Yes. She and her husband are alive and very well."

Two days later it was announced in one of the Tehran papers that Clara's friend was going to be put on trial next fall for various issues related to national security. From Clara herself there was perfect silence, except for an e-mail that Malek had received when she was safely back in the States: *Contact US embassy in the Emirates for your mother's visa.* No blockbuster news about her time in jail. Not even an article or interview. Silence. That day, when he returned to the room where she was handcuffed, he had set the photograph of her and The Man on the steel table and waited for her response.

"You took this?" she asked, staring up at him.

"Jesus, Clara! How would I take it? They also have ones of me and you. I just saw those."

"What do they want?"

"Your quiet. They don't need you to go in front of their cameras here and confess that you are a foreign agent inciting rebellion. They won't require you to do anything. They just want you to shut up and go away and never come back to this place. Do you think you can do that?"

Her body trembling, she'd answered, "Yes, I can do that. I swear to God I can do it."

"One other thing."

She looked at him with worry.

"Don't fear, *my love*," he said casually, "I just need a favor. You have contacts in Washington. And I have a mother."

Maman had cleaned up her act. But it was a forced cleanup, and she didn't seem too happy about it. During the midsummer political arrests, her heroin park had fallen to the onslaught of the police. She and her crew had been sent to various three-week camps where they had to kick the habit cold turkey. She looked slightly fattened up and irritable. She would stay clean for another two days at most, then one morning, just as easily as sipping a glass of tea, she'd pick up a spoon and aluminum foil and prepare her dosage. That was how it always went after a forced cleanup.

Malek gave her the Toblerone chocolate he'd brought for her.

With her usual toothless half grin, she started sucking on a piece of the chocolate right away. "Do you know, Aqa Reza, health is something that is like language. I don't know this language very well. But I know how to be sick. I am comfortable in sickness." She glanced away from her bench at a pair of policemen passing nearby. They waved at her. Her friends. They'd arrest her one day and shout greetings the next. "Our land is the same, you know. It only knows how to be sick."

Malek handed her a key. She examined it and put it inside the fold of her *chador*.

"It is for the Afghan, Maman *jaan*."

"I hear he is still not around the neighborhood."

"You hear right. The key, it's to a house he bought from me. From my mother, actually. I didn't want to give it to anyone but him. See that he gets it."

"You are going away again?"

"For good this time."

"You are leaving the sickness behind."

He gave her some money. "I will visit you again before leaving."

"Go with God. Our times here are not changing."

"In the streets they say the opposite; they say everything is changing."

"The streets fool themselves. There is no new revolution. And even if there were, I would want no part of it.

Revolution is not my language. It carries hope, which is a false husband. I've had my share of those."

Malek nodded. He would have liked to bring James McGreivy to this park one day to meet Maman. James would have appreciated her. Her philosophy. Her tired wisdom. She was Iran in a nutshell. She wasn't going anywhere.

"Go with God!" she shouted again after him.

James had sent him pictures in an e-mail. San Francisco. A cable car going down that hill toward Fisherman's Wharf. Candace Vincent and her kids hanging off the side of the cable car smiling at the camera, happy. James wrote that he'd already managed to create a veteran's group in Oakland to help former soldiers get jobs and go back to school. Pretty soon he'd be shuttling back and forth to DC to lobby the government for his new organization. But Oakland was where he meant to stay. He even had teaching offers again. Small ones. *I'll be less in-your-face this time, Rez. I've learned a few things.*

When the short walk from the park brought him to Sina's place, Malek saw a brown car already parked opposite the railway tracks. Fani, who sat in the car alone, had given him the heads-up he'd promised. He didn't have to. But he had. Something had happened to Fani so that he was going out of his way to be nice to Malek. Even though the streets had been quiet of late and there were no more demonstrations set to take place until early September, Fani wasn't taking any chances. He'd called Malek often and taken him out to lunch a couple of times. He'd shown concern about Soaad's American visa and expressed satisfaction when Malek told him the visa had finally been approved. The man had even talked about his own family and brought out some authentic-looking family pictures. Malek didn't know if any of this was real or not. But the contacts between the two men were not without effect.

One day Malek had to finally ask him: "You really are concerned the Americans will show up here, aren't you?"

"Do you blame me, Malek?"

"I promise I'll put in a good word for you when *we* come."

"You have my eternal gratitude."

"Just remember, you have promised to let me know before you move in on Sina Vafa."

"You speak the words as if you have no heart, Malek, as if you do not care for him."

"I speak the words without illusion."

Malek now nodded toward the brown car in which Fani sat. Behind it, fifty meters off, there was another vehicle with two more men in it. He knew them. They were the ones who had picked him up in front of Soaad's place on the day of the last big demonstration.

He continued to the other side of the tracks. The little shop was closed. Further off, the shop boy and his friends were attempting to fly an orange-yellow kite from a rooftop. Malek felt dizzy. The midday summer heat of south Tehran made the ground seem burned into submission.

Sina's door was ajar. Malek knocked and entered without waiting for an answer.

Sina sat on the floor next to his medicine kit with a large book on his lap. He glanced up, saw Malek, and offered a big smile. "Listen to the Book: *It was WE who created man, and WE know what dark suggestions his soul makes to him.* Isn't that true poetry, Rez?"

A decade of studying the Muslim mystics returned automatically to Malek and he answered easily in Koranic Arabic, *"Not a word does man utter but there is a sentinel by him ready to take note."*

Sina lay the Koran aside and got up to embrace Malek. "Welcome, brother."

"Why read that now?" Malek asked.

"It gives me solace."

"What is it that bothers you that you need solace?"

Sina closed the door and locked it. Then he fished under the sink to gather what they needed for an opium interlude. Malek lightly protested that he hadn't come for that, but Sina paid him no mind and continued putting the charcoal together.

Strange how the horror of it all seemed to distill itself into that charcoal burner Sina was toying with. Malek reached and forced the burner upside down so that the coal fell out and went cold in the sink.

Sina looked up. "What are you doing?"

"Who was killed instead of you in Kirkuk?"

Sina retreated to where he'd been sitting. He leafed through a few more pages of the book, murmured something to himself, and then turned to Malek who was still standing by the sink. "I already told you, the man who died in my place there, he was no angel."

"I don't suppose it was him—your lover's brother—who they killed?"

"If only it had been that murdering—" Sina swallowed his words, his voice cracking. It was a rare hint of real emotion. Malek watched him. He had to remind himself that this was a man who had known love once, and not too long ago. It had been misplaced love, with some Sunni girl in Iraqi Kurdistan in the middle of the war. It was, in fact, as misplaced a love as you could find in times like these. And when that girl's brother had killed her for it, Sina had no revenge to calm his spirit. Sina gathered himself. "No. No such luck. I will never have that satisfaction. Tehran wouldn't allow me to take him out."

"Then who was it they killed in your place?"

"No one you know, Rez. Let it rest! It was a *triple*."

Malek looked at him nonplussed. What in God's name was a triple?

Sina pressed his palms to his forehead and leaned back to stare at the ceiling. He sighed impatiently. "A triple is this: one, we got rid of someone, a real rat, who was giving us a lot of trouble over there; two, we managed to chalk the hit on the Americans; and three, I—your friend, your brother, your pal of twenty years—supposedly died in that hit and am no longer a concern to anyone. A triple, Rez. One, two, three. That's what we call it—*se-neshun*."

"And you sit here, read your holy book, give out a few worthless pills to people, teach English to poor children, and make everything okay in your head?"

The silence felt like sin. Malek had pushed the issue because he couldn't leave here not having tried. It was more for himself, he realized now, than for Sina. Not that it made a difference, but he had to believe he'd depart this place leaving no stone unturned.

He said, "I just need to know why. That's all."

"I'm spent, Rez. I got nothing more."

"Why did you agree to this operation at all?"

"Agree? I don't get to pick and choose what I do."

"But why use me to do it?"

"It just happened that way. You have to believe me. I only asked you to come to Tehran because of two women. So, tell me . . . how is she?"

"Your mother is all right. I have taken care of her."

"And your own?"

"Soaad is okay too. I thank you for her. For calling me here. For saving her."

"I'm not all evil then, you see!"

Malek took a deep breath. "One of those Basra Sufis once said, *Crush one ant and it's like you slaughtered a thousand men.*"

"And you've never crushed an ant, I suppose?"

"Not knowingly."

"Sure. You sit in your comfortable little college in America and let GI Joe do the crushing. And you're happy your own hands are clean."

"We've been through this. A million times. I didn't come here for a political argument today, Sina."

"Then why did you come?"

"To learn the truth."

"And you feel better now that you know?"

No. He didn't. He said softly, "Listen, Sina . . . I had to sign over your estate to them. I had no choice."

"I know you didn't have a choice." He laughed weakly. "Sometimes life is like that, as I've been trying to tell you. They kill me off in Iraq, but keep me alive in Tehran until they are sure my estates are signed over. It's like the beast always needs to have its bookkeeping in order."

"Why even go to the beast in the first place?"

"Oh my friend! It's too late for me to think about all that now."

"I'm sorry then."

"Don't fret, brother. They might let me live yet. I'm no bother to anyone here." Sina opened his arms wide and attempted a smile. "Seriously, they just might let me live."

Malek turned to go. As he was leaving, he heard Sina call out, "I wish I could have been one of those Muslim mystics of yours. Wish I could have been a saint who wouldn't even crush an ant."

"No you don't."

When he emerged outside, he didn't see the cars. For a moment he felt hopeful, as if the danger had passed. He had the idea of losing himself in the Grand Bazaar of Tehran today. Soaad had told him that before becoming completely hospital-bound, Anna had insisted she wanted to visit the vast place one last time. The two women had hired a car for the day. Then, at the main entrance to the bazaar, they'd done something silly and beautiful: they'd hired a horse-and-buggy and had the driver take them up and down the newly refurbished yellow-brick boulevard as if they had been transported back sixty years. They had giggled like little children and paid the horse-and-buggy man for a second ride before Anna started coughing and had to be rushed back home.

Malek dialed America.

James McGreivy spoke loudly into his phone, "Boyo, I'm in DC getting ready to talk the ears off a couple of congressmen later today. The bastards pretend they like to listen when it comes to veterans' affairs. But I'll get a million bucks out of them, or my name's not my name."

"How's your family?"

James paused. "Fine. And you?"

Malek heard a car roll up beside him. It was Fani, with whom he locked eyes while the phone was still to his ear. He said to James, "Everything's good with me. I'll catch you in California. You'll get to see my mother." To Fani he said, "Where are your men?"

The other man stared, saying nothing.

"I need a bank check from you."

"A check?" Fani stuck his head out the window. "Want to get in? Want to go for a ride?"

"No, I don't need a ride." They were parallel to the highway and the whoosh of cars and trucks gave a false sense that there might actually be a breeze in Tehran's dead air. "What I need is a check. As in money. A check with Sina Vafa's mother's name written on it. I haven't asked you for much. I'm asking you now."

"Do you realize I have saved you from being killed, Mr. Malek?"

"Not really. You are protecting yourself. Keeping all your options open. Which is wise. You are a wise man, Fani. And soon to be a very rich wise man. So a nice sum on a check with a few zeros to the right of the first digit will not break you. I ask you this as a favor."

"You are selling your friend for the sake of a check to his mother?"

"If you like to believe that, it's all right with me."

"Get inside the car."

Malek did.

Fani turned to him. "How do you know my check will be good? Bad checks are as common as furniture in our country."

It was remarkable. He could already tell that Fani was going to hand over the check he was asking for. In the cockamamie universe of Fani and others like him, a guy like Malek who had written a book about the Middle East had to have "deep" connections in America. This was how these people thought, Malek reflected, in terms of everything having some operational value, some sequence, some link between one man to another who could save the hide of a third man someday, somewhere. And this gave Malek the courage to sit in this car and say what he had to say.

"If your check is no good, Fani, I'll know. And one day, when we Americans arrive, I will, well, forget to put in that good word for you."

Fani smiled and looked away. He wasn't angry. He was nothing. "Malek, you talk tough for a man who could have his testicles cut right here and now."

"Come on, Fani. You can afford a few zeros on a check. It's for a good cause."

"You are far too dreamy, my brother."

"Yes, lately I've come to believe that myself."

"So why not try to save your friend also, instead of just asking for a little more money for his mother?"

"Because a smart man knows who he can push, and when, and how far. And I think I've pushed you as much as I can today."

He saw Fani reaching into his inside coat pocket and for an instant fear gripped him. But the other man merely brought out a checkbook and asked, "Just how many zeros do you want?"

Malek exhaled deeply. "As many as you can spare today, brother Fani."

OSTRÓW MAZOWIECKA

A couple of Polish truckers were watching winter sports on the television. Soaad had gone upstairs to their hotel room to lie down. Outside, another gorgeous late-spring twilight slowly fell over Central Europe.

They'd made a voyage of it. In Krakow he'd watched her stand in the middle of the town's jaw-dropping central square one evening and stare like a little child. But the next day she had refused to go on a tour of the Auschwitz concentration camp with him. It had irritated him. Wasn't that what she'd wanted? Wasn't that why they were here . . . for Anna? They'd been sitting for breakfast at an outdoor restaurant in the old Jewish quarter of Kazimierz. The restaurants all advertized klezmer music at night and on the sidewalk people sold magnets with Stars of David on them.

"So where are the Jews?" she'd asked.

"Not here."

"This is all make-believe then? Like that place I saw once on TV, Madame Tussauds?"

"You could say that. The lucky ones like Anna, they got away. The others . . . well, you already know. Auschwitz is about an hour-and-a-half drive from here. You'll see it tomorrow."

She had looked him square in the eyes then. An expression of defiance clouding her face for the very first time. "I'm not coming."

"Why not?"

"I don't want to. I cannot."

But Malek hadn't insisted. It had been a good nine months. He might even say a great nine months. Soaad had taken to America right away. New York especially. As if she'd always belonged there and was just late arriving. Soon she was going on long walks in the city by herself and her already functional English gave her a measure of independence that he had not expected would arrive so soon. During winter break he had taken her to California. To Fresno, where they'd visited the old man's grave. She'd done her usual thing, laid the flowers, didn't cry, and scrubbed and cleaned the stone. She'd asked him if they had Muslim cemeteries in Fresno and he told her he didn't know and didn't care.

Throughout that year he'd return home at nights from teaching to find her watching the same Persian channels everyone watched in Tehran. She only watched news though. The demonstrations back home were over. A lot of people had been jailed or disappeared. And Clara Vikingstad's man was appealing his high-profile case to no purpose. Soaad didn't ask him about Sina. She didn't ask him much of anything that had to do with Tehran. It was as if they had shed a skin together and she didn't want them to revisit that certain geography unless it was through the television. Then, as soon as he got home, she would turn off the TV and make conversation about New York while preparing his dinner. She'd tell him about the places she'd gone that day, the people she'd seen. Sometimes she was breathless with her ideas. He had suggested to her she might study for a certificate to teach yoga here and she had beamed at the thought.

She was happy.

They were both happy.

Only two episodes had brought the two of them back to Tehran. One was that visit to his father's grave in Fresno, which she had insisted on. The second was coming here, to Poland. To Poland so that she could see where Anna was born. It was an odd request. But he'd thought, why not? He'd show her the world. They'd start with Poland. It was as good a place to start as any. Maybe he'd show her Rome afterward, or Paris. All the places she'd dreamed about her whole life. He wanted to do things for her. He liked having a mother. He liked having her there when he returned from work at night. Was this strange? One evening he'd gone out for drinks with a woman who taught in the Spanish department. He came home at three in the morning feeling guilty, thinking she'd be waiting up for him and upset. But she'd been sleeping peacefully in her bed and the next morning she didn't even bring up the subject.

So it was all really just in his own head. Everything. She had left the Islamic Republic, at last. She was grateful to him for that. And she didn't ask too many questions.

And at the college, they left him in peace now. They too were grateful. Grateful that James McGreivy was gone. In truth, James was too far gone for Malek. The regular calls had stopped a few months back. In early January, when Malek had left a message saying they would be visiting California and wanted to see them in Oakland, there had been no response. It would have been a couple hours' drive from Fresno, but James's determined silence had kept Malek away and he'd said nothing to Soaad about it.

Which made it all the more odd that James would suddenly want to see him. They had been in Warsaw, with plans to travel in a couple of days to a small town neither of them could pronounce quite right, Ostrów Mazowiecka, Anna's birthplace.

"Where are you now?" James asked on the phone.

"With my mother. In Poland."

"Poland?"

"At this very moment I'm showing her a monument to the battle of Monte Cassino. Why haven't you answered my calls, James?"

"I'm calling you now. I want to see you."

"I'll be back in New York soon."

"No. I want to see you now."

"Then you'll have to fly to Poland."

"All right, I will."

So Malek waited. James had already called to say he'd landed at the Warsaw airport and when Malek told him they were in Ostrów, he'd said he could be there by late afternoon.

But this was a day that finally exhausted Soaad. The guidebooks said nothing about this place. Ostrów was just another no-face town where almost every single Jew had been killed seventy years ago. Like a good son, Malek had diligently researched the place, so when Soaad asked to see the town's Jewish cemetery he found himself guiding them and their hired driver to a place that was nothing more than a massive asphalted-over area where they held a livestock market on weekends. Malek had no idea what his mother had expected to find here. But after all the cemeteries they'd been to together, seeing something that was not even a ruin, not even a desecration, but a complete absence, a farce, a nonexistence—a livestock market, for the love of God— was a real punch to the gut. And Malek had seen his mother practically wilt under the knowledge of what this town had done to Anna's people. He had never seen her like this. Even in their worst moments in Tehran she had always remained a trooper. But now something gave and Malek thought if he didn't take her back to their hotel right away he'd have to find her a hospital.

The hotel waitress came around with four shots of vodka and two beers on a tray. She smiled questioningly at Malek and laid all the drinks on the table. Malek turned around to find James downing a shot at the bar before coming to the table.

He looked as healthy as ever and had shaved off his hair. He could have been a Polish policeman.

Malek downed two of the shots without getting up to say hi. James downed the other two and immediately started on his beer even before sitting down.

"What?" Malek asked.

James held four fingers to the waitress. Four more shots.

"Why the rush to come to . . . Ostrów Mazowiecka?"

"What are you doing here?"

"I'm giving my mother a tour of the places in Europe with blood on their hands."

"Then it's going to be a very long tour."

Malek said nothing.

"Where's your mother?"

"She's upstairs. Resting. We didn't have such a good day."

"Blood on their hands . . ." McGreivy murmured.

"Why are you here, James? This is too odd."

"Who was it we killed in Kirkuk?"

"What?"

"You know what."

Malek allowed himself to drift. Darkness was taking a long time to come outside. And how inordinately beautiful it was just then. The curlicues of clouds and the lingering pink sky transported him back to that day he had stood with his mother in the south of Tehran laying flowers on Anna's made-up grave. A year and a half later, here they were, in Anna's town. And something about the quality of the two twilights, so far apart, was exactly the same. It was as if the hour was giving homage to their lost Anna one last time.

The Polish truckers paid their bill and retired upstairs. The waitress played with the remote until she found some live music on the TV. In a corner of the desolate restaurant an old couple were eating their dessert in silence. This hotel was like a monument to ordinariness. Except that a half-hour drive away at the Treblinka death camp the Nazis had murdered some 850,000 people. When Malek had asked their dapper driver, proud of his mint-condition BMW taxi, if he'd ever been to Treblinka, he'd said no. It had dawned on Malek that the guy didn't even know what the place was. And didn't care.

Who did we kill in Kirkuk? He'd asked the very same question of Sina.

Maybe he'd get up early in the morning and go to Treblinka by himself. He'd read in the guidebooks that it wasn't anything like the awful tourist trap at Auschwitz that he'd ended up visiting alone. Yes, he'd do that. He'd go without Soaad again. His mother had had enough of this place. The Polish people had been gracious and polite and good to them. He wanted her to take that feeling away with her from this trip, and not the unrighteous parking lot where the townsfolk sold their livestock.

"What have you been up to this year?"

James went along with the change of subject. "I'm back and forth to Washington. I may have to move the family back to the East Coast."

"The family is good?"

"Excellent. And you?"

"Teaching. The college administration is so happy you're gone that I think I could walk naked to my classes and they wouldn't care. You cemented my career for me, mate."

"Then tell me who died instead of your friend in the Kirkuk operation. I've come a long way, Rez, to find out. I couldn't sleep on it anymore."

Malek now understood that it was a question James McGreivy had wrestled with for at least half a year. At some point the kernel of doubt had popped into his head and then his soldier's soul wouldn't leave him alone about it. Yet he had continued with his daily life and taken care of the kids and been good to Candace and hustled those politicians in Washington, and all the time this doubt had festered. Then one day, when he couldn't stand it any longer, he had called Malek and flown on a red-eye flight, all the way to this five-cent town in Central Europe, to confront Malek about it.

It was as good a place as any to do this.

Malek said, "The fellow who got killed in Kirkuk was, I'm told, some bad guy."

"But it wasn't your friend."

"Right. Not him."

"Why did you do it, Rez?" The voice asking was full of hurt; there was no anger in it though. It had distance from a deed that had been done and finished. It was almost wistful.

Malek looked outside where the lights at the gas station across the street had finally come on. He would have liked James to meet his mother. Maybe that would explain a few things; but maybe it wouldn't.

"You got pulled into this, didn't you?

"Yes," Malek answered quietly. "How did you figure it out?"

"It took me awhile. Then I thought, Reza Malek is not the type of man to give someone away, especially not a friend, not even a friend gone nasty in Iraq. I recalled the number they tried to pull on you at the college. You took a hit for me."

"Does anyone else know?"

"No one else will ever know. As you say, some other bad guy was taken out in your friend's place. At the end of the day, the accounting is all the same. One bad guy here, one bad guy there. Who cares, right?"

"Sina Vafa, he wasn't so bad."

"You speak of him in past tense."

"He's dead."

James smiled. "Are you sure?"

It had been a long time since Malek had thought

about this. Was he sure? "I'm not sure of anything." After a pause he asked, "Will you turn me in?"

"Turn you in to who? And for what? I got nothing."

"Thanks."

"I don't turn in a friend."

"Is that some Marine Corps thing?"

"No. It's James McGreivy. I don't betray a friend."

"But I betrayed you."

"You didn't. You fell into something. And we were both played. And it's okay. Worse things have happened in Kirkuk. I know this from first-hand experience."

"Now what?"

"Maybe you find out if your friend is really dead."

"Does it make a difference to you if he is?"

James motioned to stand up, but remained at the table.

Malek asked again, "Does it make a difference to you?"

"I don't know. Depends if I know for sure that he's neutralized now, or if he's still doing what he was doing in Iraq before all this."

Neutralized. What did that mean? This was a way of speaking that made everything seem like a diversion.

"I don't know if he's neutralized. My hunch is that he is."

James started at him: "Tell me you're sure."

There was a long pause.

James now stood up and the waitress finally came with the stuffed cabbage plate Malek had ordered forty-five minutes ago. It looked homemade; Soaad and Anna would have approved. James waited for her to set the plate down and leave, and then he too began to slowly shuffle away.

Malek called out to James, "Will we be seeing each other again?"

There was that same wistful look from the former captain as he turned around. "No."

"Why not?"

"It's like the war. The balance sheets are in and everyone, more or less, has to feel satisfied about it. Except you and me, Rez. And there's not a damn thing we can do about that."

Malek watched James leave through the restaurant window. He'd had a car waiting this whole time to take him back to Warsaw.

When Malek finally went upstairs two hours later, Soaad was lying in her bed. There was only a dim reading light on the side table, but he could see that her eyes were wide open and she was awake.

She said, "Let's leave this country first thing in the morning."

"You think Anna is satisfied we came here?"

"This was never her place."

"It wasn't, was it?"

She flicked the light off. He heard her praying. Till now he had thought that besides the few light trappings of her yoga practice, there was not a whole lot of religion in her. Now he heard her quietly whispering the words for the dead. Her voice soft but resolute. Malek closed his eyes, listening in the darkness to the lilting Arabic of his mother, this onetime godless Communist. He noticed she was choosing and skipping from various verses of the second chapter of the holy book, *al-Baqarah*. It was like a lullaby to his ear and he began to feel heavy with sleep. *"Our Lord, burden us not with that which we have no ability to bear. And pardon us; and forgive us; and have mercy upon us. You are our protector."*

She spoke to him: "You know, more than anything, Anna was a child of Tehran."

"All right," he whispered back.

"She never belonged here."

"No."

"Please, let's leave this place in the morning."

"All right."

They were silent for a while and then he asked her if she would recite three more times just that last verse of *al-Baqarah* for him so he could fall asleep with it. And she said yes, she would, and began the recitation for her son.

Also available from Akashic Books

TEHRAN NOIR
edited by Salar Abdoh
336 pages, trade paperback, $15.95

The Akashic Noir Series' foray into the Middle East moves unapologeti-cally forward with an unflinching noir exploration of one the world's most volatile cities. Most the writers are still living in Tehran, so this is not the "outsider's perspective" that often characterizes contemporary literature set in Iran.

BRAND-NEW STORIES BY: Gina B. Nahai, Salar Abdoh, Lily Farhadpour, Azardokht Bahrami, Yourik Karim-Masihi, Vali Khalili, Farhaad Heidari Gooran, Aida Moradi Ahani, Mahsa Mohebali, Majed Neisi, Danial Haghighi, Javad Afhami, Sima Saeedi, Mahak Taheri, and Hossein Abkenar.

THE LUMINOUS HEART OF JONAH S.
by Gina B. Nahai
432 pages, hardcover, $29.95, trade paperback, $16.95

"Gina B. Nahai has written a brilliant, funny, poignant, and thrill-ing novel about an Iranian Jewish family's struggle to find its identity in exile in America. Part murder mystery, part comic novel, *The Luminous Heart of Jonah S.* is a book you will not be able to put down."   —Reza Aslan, author of *Zealot* and *No god but God*

"Gina B. Nahai uses her gift for storytelling to add to the pantheon of American immigrant tales, but this time with an Iranian Jewish twist. This novel not only entertains, but asks the bigger question: do immigrants reinvent themselves in America or simply live out their destinies?"   —Firoozeh Dumas, author of *Funny in Farsi*

"A skilled and inventive writer."   —*New York Times Book Review*

THE PRICE OF ESCAPE
by David Unger
224 pages, trade paperback original, $15.95

"Evoking both Kafka and Conrad, Unger's character study of a broken man in a culture broken by a ravenous corporation makes compelling reading."   —*Booklist*

"Unger does a great job with fish-out-of-water situations, as [protago-nist] Samuel's travails—sometimes Kafkaesque, sometimes Laurel and Hardy—nicely pit his timidity against his growing desperation."   —*Publishers Weekly*

"David Unger's tale utterly seduces with its mix of the exotic and the familiar."   —*Toronto Star*

TEL AVIV NOIR
edited by Etgar Keret & Assaf Gavron
translated by Yardenne Greenspan
288 pages, hardcover, $26.95, trade paperback, $15.95

Though sometimes overshadowed internationally by Jerusalem, Tel Aviv is in many ways the cultural capital of Israel, and is home to many of the country's best writers. This unparalleled collection gives insight into the daily life of Israelis, albeit through a noir lens.

BRAND-NEW STORIES BY: Etgar Keret, Gadi Taub, Lavie Tidhar, Deakla Keydar, Matan Hermoni, Julia Fermentto, Gon Ben Ari, Shimon Adaf, Alex Epstein, Antonio Ungar, Gai Ad, Assaf Gavron, Silje Bekeng, and Yoav Katz.

ISTANBUL NOIR
edited by Mustafa Ziyalan & Amy Spangler
250 pages, trade paperback original, $15.95

BRAND-NEW STORIES BY: Müge İplikçi, Behçet Çelik, İsmail Güzelsoy, Lydia Lunch, Hikmet Hükümenoğlu, Riza Kiraç, Sadik Yemni, Bariş Müstecaplioğlu, Yasemin Aydinoğlu, Feryal Tilmaç, Mehmet Bilâl, İnan Çetin, Mustafa Ziyalan, Jessica Lutz, Tarkan Barlas, Algan Sezgintüredi, and others.

"The authors do an excellent job introducing readers to a city unknown to many American readers, exploring the many issues of religion and culture that face modern Istanbul. Landscape is essential to these stories, all of which convince the reader that they couldn't possibly have been set anywhere other than Istanbul." —*Booklist*

THE DESCARTES HIGHLANDS
by Eric Gamalinda
320 pages, trade paperback original, $15.95

"*The Descartes Highlands*, an amazing work of brutal candor girded by a philosopher's calm, entwines our present despair with the horrific pasts we will not escape. Eric Gamalinda's novel delivers a commitment to beauty as unflinching as the bleak truths it tells ... offering in turn what seems our only, paradoxical hope: the pained telling of our story—a gorgeous and bitter feast."
—Gina Apostol, author of *Gun Dealers' Daughter*

These books are available at local bookstores.
They can also be purchased online through www.akashicbooks.com.
To order by mail send a check or money order to:

AKASHIC BOOKS
232 Third Street, Suite A115, Brooklyn, NY 11215
www.akashicbooks.com, info@akashicbooks.com

(Prices include shipping. Outside the US, add $12 to each book ordered.)